ELLA AND THE MONSTERS

ANDREW S. FRENCH

NEONOIR BOOKS

ALSO BY ANDREW S. FRENCH

The Arcane Supernatural Thriller Series

Book one: The Arcane

Book two: The Arcane Identity

Book three: The Arcane Quest

Book four: The Arcane Ultimatum

The Ella Finn Fantasy Novella Series

Ella and the Elementals

Ella and the Multiverse

Ella and the Monsters

Ella and the Dreamers

Supernatural Short Stories

Dead Souls

The Shadow

Science Fiction

The Time Traveller's Murder

The Mercy Sleep

Bodies

The Astrid Snow series

Book one: Don't Fear the Reaper

Book two: The Killing Moon

Book three: Lost in America

Book four: Gone to Texas

Book five: The Final Girl

The Detective Jen Flowers series

Book one: The Hashtag Killer

Book two: Serial Killer

Book three: Night Killer

Book four: The Killer Inside Them

Northern Crime Fiction

Where The Bodies Are Buried

The Ophelia Red series

Book one: Ophelia Red

Crime Short Stories

Call Me: An Astrid Snow Short Story

Dark Snow: An Astrid Snow Short Story

Bette Davis Eyes: Detective Flowers Short Story

Go to www.andrewsfrench.com for more information.

1 FREAKY FRIDAY

Ella panicked when she saw the police car outside the house.

She sprinted towards it, rushing past the neighbours washing their cars. The smell of freshly cut grass invaded her nose as a bee flew at her. All she focused on was the car, only flicking at the bee as it landed on her cheek. The shock of it made her miss the bike someone had left lying in the street. Ella's foot caught the back wheel and she went flying to the ground. Her leg hit the concrete, and she dropped her schoolbooks everywhere.

'Damn!' she said as the bee flew away.

Ella sat there, rubbing at the pain in her knee, and peered at the car again. The last time she'd come home from school and found a cop car outside the house was when her parents had disappeared. That had been eighteen months ago and when they'd lived in London. Now, she was three hundred miles away in the northeast, and her family had been reunited after Ella's adventures with Elementals and a trip through the multiverse.

She pressed on her trousers and knew there was already a bruise growing underneath. A year ago, when she'd arrived back from the multiverse, she would have been able to heal herself using the Light inside her. But that Elemental energy had faded over the last twelve months, and now she had to suffer like any kid who'd fallen over.

Ella rolled up her trouser leg to make sure there was no bleeding, reluctant to get up and see why the police were here. But she knew she had to. Her leg creaked as she stood, staring at the neighbours, glad none of them had wandered over to ask how she was.

Then she picked up her books, wiped the grass from them, and limped home.

Ella stumbled into the house and dumped everything on the floor before bursting into the living room. She recognised the female police officer as Dominique Keita, the Detective Sergeant who'd interviewed her a year ago, but the stern-looking man in the suit was new to her. His steely grey eyes scrutinised Ella as her mother spoke.

'Ella, this is Detective Inspector Wexford.'

'Are you here about Ratter's murder?' Ella said.

His face never moved as DS Keita replied.

'There's been a murder?'

Gemma Finn put a hand on her daughter's shoulder.

'Someone has been poisoning pets in the neighbourhood; next door's cat and Ratter.'

DS Keita offered Ella a smile of sympathy.

'Was Ratter your friend?'

Ella nodded. 'Yes, and I left her behind.' A cocktail of guilt and anger swirled inside her.

'Left behind?' Keita said.

With her heart thumping against her ribs, Ella steadied

herself, making sure not to tell them how she'd travelled to the multiverse to battle an ancient being set on conquering the Earth.

'I went on holiday without Ratter, and when I got back, she was dead.'

In her grief, Ella had considered using the power inside her, the Light, to resurrect Ratter, until she imagined bringing back a zombie rat and thought better of it.

As memories of Ratter ran through her mind, Detective Inspector Wexford opened his mouth.

'No, Ella, we're not here about a dead rat.' He gazed right through her. 'We're investigating the disappearance of your aunt, uncle and their three children.'

Gemma Finn pulled her daughter close to her.

'We've been through this before with the police several times.' She glanced at DS Keita. 'Dominique knows everything.'

Wexford removed a notebook from his jacket pocket.

'It's been a year, Mrs Finn, since your sister and her family vanished. And now Alan Twist, George Twist's brother, has made a complaint regarding your conduct and his brother's house.'

DS Keita intervened. 'He claims your husband Andrew punched him over a dispute about the property.'

The inside of Ella's head felt like a volcano, ready to explode.

'That's a lie. Dad never touched him.'

She glared at Wexford as he wrote something in his notebook.

'We have to investigate every complaint made to us.' He smiled at Ella. 'We can't have the taxpayers moaning they're not getting their money's worth from the police, can we?'

'What's an argument got to do with my sister's disappearance?' Gemma said.

Wexford's voice was like a train rumbling towards them.

'I understand there's a dispute regarding the ownership of the house since the disappearance of the Twist family.'

Ella watched as her mother's hand shook.

'There's no dispute on my part. The house is there for my sister for when she and her family return.'

'And you know nothing of what happened to them a year ago?' Wexford said.

Gemma Finn puffed out her cheeks.

'As I've already said, I've told this to the police before.'

Wexford stared at her before nodding to his colleague. Keita removed her notebook.

'The last sighting of your sister and her family was in Saltburn last year, June 2nd.' Ella waited for Wexford to mention the extraordinary events of that date, the day the world changed forever. But he didn't, instead peering right at Ella's mother as Keita continued. 'Six months before that, you and your husband Andrew also disappeared.' Wexford glanced at Ella. 'Leaving your daughter with your sister and her family four miles from here in Saltburn.'

Ella looked at her mother, hoping she'd still remember the lie Ella had convinced her parents to believe about when Pandora had abducted them.

Gemma Finn sighed. 'It was regrettable we had to deceive Ella, to put her through such trauma, but we were working on a secret government project that required drastic measures.' She touched Ella's arm. 'Andrew and I will always have that on our conscience, but it was unavoidable.'

Ella's heart ached as she stared at her mother, knowing

one day she'd be able to ease her parents' guilt by revealing what happened with their abduction.

Wexford trawled through his notebook.

'This was with Artemis, the organisation you worked for? They focus on improving living conditions in developing countries, don't they?' He didn't wait for a reply. 'That hardly seems like top-secret government work.'

Gemma smiled at him. 'Are you encouraging me to break the Official Secrets Act, Inspector?'

He shook his head. 'We're here to speak to Ella.'

'Why?' Ella said.

Wexford sat down and Ella knew the police wouldn't be leaving in a hurry.

'We have several witness reports of unusual sightings of you, Ella, on the day the Twist family disappeared.'

'Unusual?' Gemma Finn said.

'There's a report of Ella on the beach with her friends, Billy and Dora.'

'What's unusual about that?' Gemma said.

Keita checked her notebook. 'We can't trace Dora Moore.'

'She went to see her family in Greece,' Ella said.

Somewhere in the multiverse.

'What about the others you were with?' Wexford said.

Ella knew he was trying to trick her, but she stayed calm.

'What others?'

Keita returned to her notes. 'A teenage boy and a one-eyed man.'

Gemma Finn stared at her daughter. 'A one-eyed man?'

'A cyclops,' Ella replied.

Wexford laughed. 'So you're sticking to the claim from your previous police statements?'

'Yes, I am.' Defiance seeped out of Ella. 'The weather was boiling, so I went with my friends to the beach. When we got there, we found the boy and the cyclops fighting. I guess it was the start of that day's incredible events.'

'When the monsters came,' Keita said.

Wexford laughed again. 'Well, regardless of what some are claiming happened, the first reports of these monsters in the UK were from Saltburn, and you appear to be at the centre of those strange happenings, Ella.'

Ella peered at him. 'Don't you believe wondrous creatures visited the world on that day, Inspector?'

He placed his notebook on the coffee table.

'I've seen the videos, read the reports and can say it's no different from people who've reported seeing spaceships and claimed to have been abducted by aliens the last seventy years.'

'Not everyone thinks the same as you, Inspector.' Gemma Finn removed a piece of paper from her pocket. 'Somebody pushed this through our front door today.'

Wexford took it from her and gave it a cursory glance before placing it next to his notebook on the table.

Ella reached over and grabbed it.

'Destroy All Monsters.' She read the words below the heading and the poorly drawn image of a dragon attacking a ship. 'Visit www.dam.com to discover what the GOVERN-MENT is hiding from YOU about the attack on our country on June 2nd. Monsters exist, and we need to stand together to rid them from Great Britain and the World.'

Ella's fingers trembled as she finished reading. 'Is this real?'

Wexford grimaced. 'They're just a bunch of nuts; take no heed of them.' He crossed his legs. 'But back to the reason we're here, Ella. This so-called cyclops you saw on the beach that day, don't you think it might have been someone dressed up in a costume, like from a TV show or a movie?'

'Why would they do that?' Gemma said.

The Inspector stared at her. 'To spread terror, Mrs Finn. To scare the good citizens of Britain, so some will get involved in stupid things like those DAM idiots. That whole day and what followed destabilised the country and terrorised the people, using an elaborate hoax of monsters and mythological creatures come to life to divide us all.'

His voice never wavered as he spoke, but Ella saw the mania in his eyes.

Ella's mother laughed. 'Is that the official policy of the British Police, Inspector?'

He stared at her. 'You're a scientist, Mrs Finn. Are you telling me you believe in monsters?'

'There are more things in Heaven and Earth than we'll ever know, Inspector.'

Ella looked at her mother, surprised at her words.

Does she remember some of what happened to her and Dad when Pandora took them from me?

'Do you know something we don't, Mrs Finn?' Wexford said. 'Is it to do with the secret government mission you were on when you abandoned Ella and let her believe you and her father were dead?'

Ella didn't know if Wexford had meant to hurt with those words, but they sent stabs of pain through her heart as she spoke.

'I wasn't sure who they were on the beach. I only realised it was a cyclops when I saw the TV later and watched what was happening all over the world.' She glared at Wexford. 'I suppose you think it must be a worldwide conspiracy, then?'

Before he could reply, Gemma intervened.

'Ella's told you what happened on that day many times, so will you leave now?'

Wexford removed a phone from his pocket and handed it to Gemma.

'Can your daughter explain this video, Mrs Finn?'

Ella sat with her mother across from the Inspector, and they watched the clip together. Ella didn't need to see it again since the events were still vivid in her memory: her, Billy and Dora leaving the carnival in Redcar with her cousins on the way to the hospital. And the unicorn they took with them.

Then that clip ended and they were outside the hospital, pushing through a crowd surrounding the unicorn, led by a tall, dark-haired woman in a smart suit.

When the clip finished, Gemma returned the phone to Wexford.

'Ella's already explained this.'

Wexford smiled. 'Yes, I've read the reports, but I'd like to hear it in your daughter's own words, Mrs Finn.'

Gemma shook her head, but Ella answered.

'We were at the carnival in Redcar. My cousins were there, upset because their sister was in a coma. So we went and visited her. Dolly wanted to bring that fake unicorn with us. It was only a pony with a horn stuck to its bonce. Those people were confused by it outside the hospital.' Ella grinned at Wexford. 'I guess a lot of people are easily confused nowadays.'

'And your cousin, Dotty, had a miraculous recovery after your visit,' Keita said.

'The NHS is a national treasure,' Ella replied.

'And this was all before your encounter with the fake cyclops on the beach?' Wexford said.

Ella nodded. 'The day before, I think.'

'And you don't believe these encounters had anything to do with the disappearance of your cousins and their parents?'

Ella shrugged. 'Everything was strange then, especially those few days.'

Wexford turned his phone towards them and Ella saw the image frozen on the screen.

'And you claim not to recognise this woman leading you out of the hospital?'

Ella shook her head. 'She was in front of us when we heard the noises outside. That's all I know.'

Not that she's Seraphina, the witch, and she pulled Dotty out of the coma after I promised never to send Seraphina back to the Elemental world. Or that she betrayed me. And I don't know where she is.

The Inspector put his phone away. 'What happened after you moved into the crowd?'

Ella rubbed her hands as if she was bored and not trying to hide the tremble in her fingers.

'We ran out the other side and went home.'

Wexford sat in silence for two minutes. Ella expected him to jump up and slap the handcuffs on her. But he grabbed his notebook and stood.

'We still need to speak to your husband, Mrs Finn, regarding the claim of an altercation between him and Alan Twist.'

'He's working on the allotment today,' Gemma said. 'I'll get him to come to the police station, shall I?'

Wexford nodded. 'As soon as possible, Mrs Finn, as soon as possible.'

Ella watched her mother lead them out of the house and wondered, not for the first time, what had happened to the Twist family.

And she promised herself she'd find out.

2   THE GARDEN OF EARTHLY DELIGHTS

Once the police left, Ella went into the back garden. She took a single rose from the flowers in the kitchen on her way, placing it under her nose and breathing in its sweet aroma. She stood near the table and chairs on the patio, letting the sun caress her face. Smoke came over the fence from next door, and she knew the neighbours had a barbecue going.

Ella scrunched up her face at the smell and strode through the garden, surprised at how many weeds were there and wondering why her parents had let them get so unruly. A bee flew towards the rose in her hand and she dodged its approach, pondering if it was the same one from before. Even though her Light had disappeared, and she still wasn't sure if that was a good or bad thing, she'd noticed on her return from the multiverse how she attracted some insects and animals to her like a magnet.

She kept a careful eye on the bee as it flew over the trees, with her mind focused on one animal now: Ratter. Ella approached the grave under the wooden seat in front of the fence, bending her legs to put the rose on the spot where she'd buried her friend a year ago.

'I know you're in a better place, girl, but I wish I could have saved you.' She stared at her hands as the gravel bit into her knees. 'All that power I had, and I couldn't do anything for you.'

Ella fought back the tears, feeling the pain in her heart as she went to stand.

Then she saw the earth twisting in front of her. The shock of it made her legs buckle, and she flopped onto her backside. The tiny stones sent a sharp stab through her, but she couldn't take her eyes off the ground moving towards her.

Perhaps my Light has returned, and thinking about Ratter again has brought her back to life.

She clutched at her chest, her heart beating at a thousand miles a second, picturing all those zombie moves she wasn't supposed to have seen coming to life in the garden.

What will I do with a resurrected dead Ratter? Maybe she won't remember me and will try to tear my throat out or eat my brains.

As that terrible image filled her head, the moving earth got closer to her, slithering like a snake. Her ribs ached as Ella realised it wasn't a zombie rat coming for her, but a horde of black ants carrying leaves on their backs. She was glued to the ground as the insects marched past her with their trophies. Ella watched them move under the fence and into the neighbour's garden.

Her heart steadied as her breathing returned to normal before she heard the buzzing above her. Ella jumped up, her neck twisting, eyes wide with astonishment at the bees hovering over her. There must have been hundreds of them, their yellow and black bodies peering down at her as Ella's legs refused to move.

Then a hand dragged her back, and she found herself smothered against someone. She struggled to breathe before wriggling out of the unknown grasp.

The bees flew away as Ella gazed at her mother.

'Ever since the climate got mucked up, it's done strange things to the insects,' Gemma Finn said.

Ella smiled at her, but inside she let out a heavy sigh. Fixing the damage to the climate was one thing she'd promised to do when she'd discovered Elementals and Light. Elementals could use their Light to repair the damage to the environment. She'd proved this before on that day the Earth learnt magical creatures existed. So, just like the unicorn had healed people at the hospital, the Elementals Ella had summoned into the world using the Book of All Life were fixing the destruction to the environment.

But then it all went wrong.

Her ancestor, the Goddess Pandora, tricked Ella, using the book to bring evil Elementals to Earth. This was the day the police had asked her about: the day the monsters came, and her aunt, uncle, and cousins vanished.

Only those Elementals weren't evil or monsters. Ella knew they only did terrible things because Pandora had made them. And before her cousins disappeared, Pandora had used her Light to transform the three teenage girls into one giant deformed creature. Just to attack Ella and her friend, Billy.

As much as her cousins had tormented Ella from the moment she'd stepped into their house, she still felt guilty about what had happened to them.

Regardless of why the police were here, I need to search for my cousins again.

It had been one of the first things she'd done on her return from the multiverse, but no matter where she looked, without her Light, she'd found no trace of them. Staring into her mother's face now only reminded Ella of another of her failures.

I couldn't save Ratter. I can't fix the climate. And I lost my cousins and their parents.

Ella took her mother's hand. 'It's going to be a hot summer.'

Gemma made sure the bees had left before taking her daughter to sit on the bench.

'I don't want you to worry about the police coming here, Ella.'

Ella nodded. 'Will they give up looking for Aunt Ida and the others?'

Gemma squeezed Ella's fingers. 'No, I don't think so, love.' She gazed into her daughter's eyes. 'Five people can't just up and vanish like that without someone knowing something.'

'Could it have had something to do with that secret government project you and Dad were doing?'

This was the one thing Ella feared the most: that the lie she'd placed inside her parents' heads would fill them both with guilt. Her mum and dad had no memory of Pandora abducting them. So when Ella had returned from the multiverse, she'd used the last of her Light to place the fake memories in their minds to protect them from the truth.

But every day since then, Ella had worried if she'd done the right thing. It had kept the police from asking too many questions, though that could be over after today's visit. And it had allowed her parents to return to normal life without worrying about their daughter's blood connection to an ancient deity.

And not just my connection to Pandora, but Mum's as well.

No, she'd done the right thing. One day she'd tell them the truth, but that day wasn't now.

Gemma shook her head and smiled at her daughter. 'No, Ella. Your father and I were working on a project to bring clean water to Africa. The government only deemed it secret because some places we worked in were... well, not to worry you, but they were war-torn countries. And the fewer people who knew we were there, the better.'

Ella returned her mother's smile. Her parents had been working on clean water systems for Africa, but they'd only spent a week on the continent before returning home to London. And that was when Pandora spirited them away and kept them in a state where they couldn't remember what had happened to them.

But it meant Ella had a grain of truth to work on when she'd implanted the false memories in their heads.

'What do you think happened to Aunt Ida, Mum?'

Gemma Finn's smile disappeared. 'My sister has never been one to face responsibility head-on, Ella. So I'm guessing once she knew of your father and me returning, she couldn't stand seeing me, knowing how I'd respond to what she and her family did to you in that place in Salt-burn.' Ella saw the anger in her mother's eyes. 'I'm sure she'll come back to sort that house out. I can't see her leaving the property so George's brother can get his grubby hands on it.'

Ella laughed. 'Did Dad really punch him?'

Her mother grinned. 'Alan Twist? Your father is not a man of violence, but it's fair to say he's never got on with any of the Twists. I think it started at Ida's wedding when he argued with Alan, and it only got worse over the years.'

'What were they arguing about?'

Gemma shook her head. 'It was something to do with music, or football, or some other trivial nonsense. Of course, your father had forgotten about it by the next day, but the Twist brothers are people who like to hold grudges. It's one reason why we rarely visited your cousins over the years.'

'Didn't you miss seeing your sister, Mum?'

A wistful look crossed Gemma Finn's face. 'Ida and I have never been close, Ella. I'm not sure why that is. It might have had something to do with your grandparents favouring me over her, as Ida always claimed, but it could be as simple as the fact we're just two completely different people. We have nothing in common apart from our blood.'

Yes, our heritage and bloodline that stretches down through the centuries and right back to Pandora. At least, that's what Pandora told me.

'Is that why I'm an only child?'

Gemma jerked up. 'What?'

Ella wasn't sure why those words had come out of her mouth, but she couldn't stop herself.

'Not getting on with your sister. Is that why I haven't got a brother or sister?'

Her mother pulled at the collar of her top, and Ella watched her cheeks flush.

'No, Ella, of course not. Your father and I, we just... well, work got in the way for a long time, and now...'

'Now I'm too old.'

Gemma held Ella's hand. 'You're fourteen soon, which

isn't old at all.' She ran her fingers through her daughter's hair. 'Would you like to have a brother or sister?'

Ella shrugged. 'I don't know. Maybe.'

Gemma grinned. 'Well, okay. You think about it, and I'll have to talk to your father.'

Ella thought about it.

If I have a brother or sister, will they have Light in them as well? I guess not, since I only got it from the Elementals I connected with. And the real power came from Pandora, and that was because she's my ancestor. My mother doesn't have Light, and it was the same with her sister and my cousins.

Gemma Finn led her daughter into the house as Ella considered what to do next. She left her mother in the kitchen and ran upstairs to her bedroom. She changed out of her school clothes and pulled on a pair of jeans and a clean top. Then she reached under the bed and removed the Book of All Life from its secret hiding place.

Ella sat on the carpet with her back pushed against the bed. She placed one hand on the rug and rested the other on the front cover of the book. She'd have a better chance of finding her missing cousins, aunt and uncle if she could replenish the Light she'd lost. And she could only do that if she used the book to summon more Elementals to Earth.

She stared at the illustrations on the cover, as she had every day for the past year. Ella ran her finger over them, touching the images of the dragon, the wizard, the gorgon, the elf, and the mermaid, before stopping on the one of a witch.

A witch could help me find the Twists.

But she'd brought a witch over before: Seraphina.

Seraphina who'd betrayed Ella, and who worshipped at the feet of Pandora.

So how could she trust another witch?

Ella's finger hovered over the illustration of the witch, wondering if she should take the risk.

Was it worth it to discover what had happened to her relatives?

3   HERE COMES THE SUN

Ella's finger was lingering over the illustration of the witch when the phone rang. She dropped the Book of All Life on the floor and jumped up to get her mobile. She grabbed it from the table and answered it.

'I'll meet you at the pier in thirty minutes, Billy.'

Her best friend, Billy Pudding, laughed down the line. 'You can't cycle from your house to Saltburn in half an hour, Ella.'

'How do you know I'm at home?'

She imagined him grinning on the other end. 'Because you're not long out of school, and you won't leave before you've stuffed your face.'

'That's where you're wrong, Mr Pudding. I haven't had time for my tea yet.' Should she tell him about the police visit? Maybe later. 'You're only jealous because I'm faster on a bike than you.'

'When you get here, I'll race you up the bank, and then we'll see who's the fastest.'

Ella laughed and hung up. Then she returned the Book

of All Life to its hiding spot and ran downstairs to let her mother know where she was going.

Gemma Finn was in the kitchen slicing some carrots. 'Visit your father at the allotment on your way. Tell him to bring some eggs back with him.'

Ella grabbed an apple from the side and took a bite. 'Okay, Mum. Should I mention the police visit?'

Her mother put down the knife. 'No, leave that to me. I'll explain it to him later.'

Ella nodded before leaving and getting her mountain bike from the garage. She finished the apple and slipped the core into her pocket. Then she rode off, in no hurry to make the journey in thirty minutes like she'd promised Billy since she knew she'd be talking to her father at the allotment.

She cycled from Redcar into Marske over the bridge, enjoying the effort it put into her legs and feeling her muscles come alive. Ella kept off the road, riding along a cycle path for most of the way before it ended and she moved onto the pavement. Then she cut through a pub car park and into one of the quieter roads of the estate. When she came out, she crossed over at the school and took the route near the sea. This ran parallel with the train line and led into Saltburn allotments.

Ella enjoyed the sun on her face and the wind in her hair, glancing at St Germain's Churchyard on her left as she went. Beyond that, she saw the water on the horizon, noticing the ships there as they waited to enter Tees' dock. Billy had told her they should cycle out there one day to look at the ships close up. One thing Ella had always wanted to do was go out to sea and, even though she only lived a few minutes from the coast, she hadn't done it yet.

That thought drifted through her mind as she cycled up the slight incline towards Saltburn. But Ella was concentrating so much, she didn't notice the darkness above her. It was only as a bus overtook her she noticed the shadow descend.

Damn. I should have worn my hoody if it's going to rain.

Then she glanced up and saw no clouds hanging above her, but a large group of gulls.

Ella put her head down and cycled as fast as she could, ignoring the birds. There were no other people around as she entered the narrow cycle path and gripped the handlebars. There was a field of cows to her left as she slowed along the narrowest part of the route. Even though she didn't look up, Ella knew the birds were still following her. The shadow of the gulls dropped until it was closer to her than she wanted it to be.

Ella slammed on the brakes, skidding through the small stones as her heart thumped against her ribs. Then she jerked up, and the gulls scattered around her. Most of them squawked at her before flying high into the sky, all apart from two sitting on the wire fence separating the path from the field. They peered at her through yellow eyes as dozens of cows gathered behind them.

Is this something to do with me or the changes in the climate?

She sat there on the bike, staring at the animals as they scrutinised her. Were Elementals controlling the birds and cows as one of them, Fazzlepuff, had done with Ratter when Ella discovered the Book of All Life?

Ella stared at the biggest cow, thinking of the talking cows she'd met on the moon in the multiverse.

'Do you want to tell me something?' she said.

They were silent, but the birds twisted their heads to look at each other. Then they opened their mouths and Ella waited for them to speak.

But all they did was squawk at her before lifting off the fence and joining the other gulls in the sky. They flew towards the cliffs where Ella's adventures had begun eighteen months ago. The cows turned from her as well, returning to chewing the grass. Ella sat for a few seconds, watching both sets of animals go. She didn't know what was going on, but was sure it wasn't a good omen.

Ella took a deep breath and set off again, knowing she wasn't too far from the allotment where her dad was. Her phone vibrated in her pocket and she assumed it would be Billy wondering where she was. She ignored it and continued cycling.

Two minutes later, she pulled up outside the *Eggs For Sale* sign and got off the bike. She pushed it through the gate and looked for her father.

'Dad, are you here?'

Ella placed the bike against the hen house, expecting the chickens to stroll over and stare at her. Instead, they kept on picking at the feed on the ground and ignored her. Then, as she glanced at them, everything went dark around her.

She wriggled away from the fingers over her eyes and turned to scowl at her father.

Andrew Finn grinned at her. 'I didn't think you were frightened so easily, Ella.'

Ella rubbed at her nose and grimaced. 'You haven't washed your hands, and you stink of manure.'

Her father's shoulders trembled as he laughed. 'You're in a little part of the countryside now, Ella, and that's what it smells like.'

'Mum won't be happy if you go home like that.'

He brushed the dirt from his fingers. 'I'll be clean before that. Did she send you to get me?'

Ella shook her head. 'No. I'm on my way to meet Billy, but she told me to remind you to take eggs with you.'

Her father grinned at her. 'So, you'd rather see your boyfriend than spend time with me?'

Her nails dug into Ella's palms as she scowled. 'Billy's not my boyfriend.'

Andrew Finn reached into his pocket and removed bits of feed before throwing it into the hen house.

'You see him every day at school, and then when you get home. Has your mother had *the talk* with you?'

'Dad!' Ella's cheeks burnt as blood trickled from one of her palms.

He moved towards her as she stood there. 'You're nearly fourteen, Ella. You shouldn't be afraid to talk about anything.'

'The police came to the house,' she blurted out.

The smile dropped from Andrew Finn's face. 'What? Why were they there?'

Ella unfurled her fingers and relaxed a little. 'They were asking about Aunt Ida and her family.' She didn't tell him how Inspector Wexford had spent most of his time interrogating her. 'Because it's been a year since they disappeared.'

She wiped her hands on her trousers, hoping he wouldn't see the damage she'd done to her palms.

He stepped closer and touched her shoulder.

'Are you okay, Ella?'

She nodded, feeling the anxiety seep out of her.

'I'm fine, Dad. Being on the bike always makes me feel better.' She didn't mention Billy again.

His smile was more subdued this time, but she noticed he'd relaxed a little.

'I'll have to get the tyres pumped up on my bike so we

can go out together. A nice flat ride down to the gare to see the fishing huts. And you can get a closer look at the boats and ships.'

He let go of her and she grinned at him. 'As long as you don't mind me being miles in front of you, Dad. You know I'm faster than you on the bike.'

Her father lifted his hand and gave her a mock expression of pain. 'It will happen to you when you're as old as me.'

Ella punched him on the arm and laughed. 'There are years to go before that, Dad. Remember, I'm only thirteen.' She stepped away from him to leave. 'Don't forget the eggs. And don't stink too much, or Mum will kill you.'

She retrieved her bike and pushed it out of the allotment, hearing her father whistling the theme tune to *Dr Who* as she left. Ella pedalled into the town, watching the sun burning above her. It seemed redder than usual, like a gigantic orange bursting at the seams. Ella swept her father's teasing about Billy to the back of her mind, feeling the sun's rays on her face.

Ella headed towards the bank down to the beach. The sky was more red than blue or white, and it made her think of what she'd seen on the news the last few days: wildfires spreading across Europe, America and Australia; flash floods in Germany and Belgium; plus drought in Africa and Asia. She'd even watched a report about swarms of locusts devouring crops in India and parts of the Middle East. Her mother had described the scenes as biblical, and Ella knew what she meant. The changes to the environment were increasing and becoming more devastating. Most world governments were saying the right things about climate change, but Ella wondered if anything they did could improve it now.

She reached the top of the bank and squeezed on the brakes. Ella scowled as she saw someone drop rubbish to the ground and had to stop herself from shouting at them. The Finn family recycled everything they could, and she'd convinced her parents to cut out all meat products. Some kids at school laughed at her for being a vegetarian, but they were in the minority. Billy had promised he'd stopped eating meat, but she knew he had a bacon sandwich for breakfast every morning. And she didn't blame him for that. She wasn't there to force others to be like her, but she recognised the world would have to make sacrifices if humans wanted to stop the planet from fighting back at them.

And that's only if it wasn't too late.

But she could change all that.

If only she used the Book of All Life again.

4 THE HEAT IS ON

Ella got off her bike and took it down to the pier to escape the sun. The excessive heat had kept the tourists away, and she saw only a few people hanging around outside the fish and chip shop.

She stepped into the shade as Billy moved out of it.

'I said you wouldn't get here in thirty minutes.'

She stuck her tongue out at him as if she was ten again.

'I stopped off to see my dad; otherwise, I'd have been here sooner.'

Billy inched towards her, and she noticed he wasn't wearing any shoes or socks. He dipped his toes into the sea.

'I swear it's getting warmer every summer here.'

Ella followed his lead, removing her shoes and socks and letting the waves wash over her feet. The water cooled her skin as it dribbled between her toes. She peered down at the water, expecting to see an army of crabs marching towards her.

'It's not the only weird thing going on, Billy.'

She told him about the police visit and the strange behaviour of the insects and the animals.

'It might have something to do with this.'

He handed Ella his phone. She stared at the screen, intrigued by the image of ancient gods sitting around a table in the sky, with mountains below them.

'What's MythMaker?'

Billy grinned at her. 'It's a new mobile app that allows you to be a mythical creature. I'm on there as Hercules. You should have a go, but you'll have to create an account first.'

She returned the phone to him and took out hers. 'I might as well if it takes my mind off things.'

Ella downloaded the app and created an account. Then she scrolled through the avatar choices before choosing a dark-haired woman holding a bow and arrow.

Billy peered at the screen over her shoulder. 'I thought you were going to pick Hel for a moment.' He grinned at her. 'I could just see you as the Norse ruler of the underworld.'

She kicked water over his legs. 'Thanks.'

He laughed at her. 'I know you've got a dark side, Ella.' Billy pointed at the phone. 'Who's that?'

'That's Artemis, the Greek goddess of the hunt. She was the daughter of Zeus and Leto and the protector of young women.'

Billy nodded. 'Cool. Is that why you picked her, to be the protector of women?'

'I suppose so. But Artemis was the company where my parents worked when we lived in London.'

'That's where Pandora kidnapped them from?'

'Yes. I guess I thought it was appropriate in more ways than one.'

'How are your ma and da? Are they okay with what happened?'

She shook her head at him. 'Are you still worried their

heads are going to explode after what I did to their memories?'

Billy held up his hands. 'No, of course not.' He laughed at her. 'You've been watching too many of my horror films since you got back from the multiverse. Don't let your parents find out about that.'

Ella grinned with him, wondering if he was worried she might have done something to his brain.

She peered at her phone. 'So what do you do in this game?'

He moved towards her. 'You use your avatar to travel the world and between realms in a battle of good and evil. You collect weapons, friends and allies and have to choose which side you're on.'

Ella flicked through the options in the app, looking at the rules and the settings.

'Every creature here is an Elemental.'

Billy whistled loudly. 'Do you think they're all real somewhere, living in the Elemental world or that multiverse you visited?'

'I don't see why not.' She did an alphabetical search on the avatars, finding the one she hoped wouldn't be there. Then she showed the screen to him.

'Pandora!'

Ella looked at the phone, reading over the details of the mythical woman who was her ancestor.

'Whoever designed the app has used the information from the Greek myth of Pandora, and not what she told us about what happened to her.'

'That's probably a good thing,' Billy said. 'Considering she claimed she was the Goddess who created all life on Earth and in the universe.' He kicked at the stones at his feet. 'Do you think she's still stuck in the multiverse? Or maybe she's the one causing the animals and the insects to behave strangely.'

Ella shook her head. 'I don't know.' It was another thing for her to worry about as she watched the tide ebb and flow over her toes. The water tickled her skin, and she allowed herself to relax.

Billy reached into his pocket and removed a piece of paper. 'We got this through the door today as well.'

Ella took it from him. 'Destroy All Monsters. Yeah, mum showed the police this. Inspector Wexford told me he believes Elementals are fake, and it was all set up by a terrorist group.' She peered at it. 'I guess these DAM people think Elementals are monsters to be killed.'

'Do you think Elementals are still coming here through gaps between dimensions caused by climate change?'

'They must be.' She stared at Billy, wondering if he thought she was bringing them over. 'I haven't used the Book of All Life since I went to the multiverse.'

'Maybe you should destroy it.'

His words shocked her. 'Why?'

'Then Pandora won't be able to return here. And that stops it falling into the wrong hands.'

Ella narrowed her eyes. 'Only Pandora and I can use it, so the book can't fall into the wrong hands.'

He didn't seem convinced. 'But, Ella, what if bad people force you to use the book?'

She laughed at him. 'And how would they do that?'

Billy shrugged. 'I don't know, but maybe someone might threaten to harm your parents if you won't do what they say.'

Ella wanted to say such a thing would never happen, but the thought had been stuck in the back of her head since she realised she'd lost her Light. She glanced down to see fish circling at her feet.

'Okay, that's a possibility, so perhaps I should be more proactive.'

'What do you mean?'

She felt her eyes sparkling. 'I could use the Book of All Life to summon some good Elementals here. Then I'd use them to bring back my Light and get them to repair the climate.'

Billy sighed. 'That's how all this started, Ella.' He snatched the DAM leaflet from her. 'That's why these people are putting stuff like this out, because of what happened with Pandora and you last year.' He crumpled the paper and threw it into the sea. 'You don't know what would happen if you start that all over again. Pandora might return, and we won't be able to beat her next time.'

The DAM leaflet floated on the water, refusing to sink or let the tide take it away. Ella bent her legs and scooped the paper from the fish swimming near it.

'Throwing this into the sea is bad for the environment, Billy. You know this.'

He held up his hands. 'I'm sorry, but I'm worried we'll make things worse than they already are.'

'You mean you think I'll make things worse.'

He turned from her, trudging through the water, so it swirled all around them. The fish near Ella's feet swam from her before quickly returning. She glanced down at them, seeing a long line of fish stretching to the far end of the pier.

They had to get out of there before anybody noticed what was happening.

Ella grabbed her bike and pulled it on to the beach. Billy chased after her, pushing his bike next to hers.

'I'm sorry, Ella.' She stopped and looked at him. 'Do you want to see what I've got with me?'

She wiped the sweat from her forehead and wondered how long she could stay outside in the heat.

'Is it more of your fancy sweets?'

In the last few weeks, Billy's sweet tooth had grown, and he'd started spending most of his pocket money on flavoured fudge from the chocolate shop in Saltburn. But it had made him more hyperactive and done nothing good for his teeth.

He grinned at her. 'No. It's much better than that.'

Ella returned his smile, thankful for something to distract her from what they'd talked about. She soon lost that grin when he showed her what he had.

'Cigarettes!' He was holding the packet in the shade between them so no passer-by could see what he had. 'Where did you get them?'

'They're my cousin Hannah's. She's visiting us from Leeds, and I found them in her room.'

'Your mother will kill you when your cousin tells her what you've done.'

Billy laughed. 'She can't, though. Hannah's sixteen, and you have to be eighteen to buy cigarettes in the UK.'

Ella shook the surprise from her head. 'She might beat you up instead.'

'I suppose.' He pushed the packet towards her. 'Do you want one?'

She grimaced. 'No. They're bad for you and the environment.' Ella stepped back as he inched closer to her, moving away from the cigarettes as if they were an unexploded bomb in his hand. 'Why would you want to do it?'

He removed a cigarette from the packet. 'It might make me cooler with the other kids at school.' His eyes narrowed as he looked at her. 'You know none of them like me.'

Ella shook her head. 'That's stupid, Billy. And anyway, doesn't the photo on the packet put you off?'

He stared at the image, holding it up so she could see it as well: a picture of diseased blackened lungs peered back at them.

'Yeah, but that's only if you smoke loads a day for twenty or thirty years. So a few won't hurt me.'

The heat from the sun travelled down Ella's head and through the rest of her body, diving underneath her skin until she thought her veins were about to explode. But it wasn't only that which was making her blood boil.

She dropped her bike on to the beach and snatched the packet from him.

'I won't let you do it, Billy.'

'Hey!' he shouted.

Ella expected him to grab them back from her, but he just stood there with his cheeks puffed out.

'It's for your own good.'

She watched his fingers turn pale as he gripped the handlebars of his mountain bike. His eyebrows wobbled as his lips trembled. Then he pushed his bike past Ella before turning to her.

'That's your biggest problem, Ella. You always think you know what's best for everyone. But you don't, do you?' His face was as red as the sun, and she saw how his breathing had increased. It was the first time she'd ever seen him lose his temper. 'This is why we have problems with Elementals now and the reason why those stupid DAM people are kicking up a fuss. All because you think you're better than everybody else.'

He turned from her and got on the bike. Then he cycled

along the sand and onto the promenade. She watched him go all the way, hoping he wouldn't fall off as he pedalled up the steep bank and to the top of Saltburn. He never looked back once and disappeared from her view.

Ella didn't move from the beach, wondering if she should send him a text and apologise.

Apologise for what? I did him a favour with his stupid cigarettes.

She slipped the packet into her trousers and pushed her bike across the sand. When she got on to the pavement, she glanced back at the sea, watching as the long line of fish undulated in the water like some giant snake.

Or sea serpent.

Was Billy right? Was everything going wrong with the environment now her fault? She'd only tried to help when bringing the Elementals here, but maybe she'd made things worse.

My meddling might have sped up the whole process of climate change.

Ella decided not to ride up the bank, using the walk to the top as time to reflect on what she'd done.

And to think about destroying the Book of All Life before things got worse.

5   SMELLS LIKE TEEN SPIRIT

Ella rose late on Saturday, not even going down for breakfast when her dad shouted for her. She had got little sleep during the night, with her head full of police visits, disappearing cousins, wild Elementals, people wearing Destroy All Monsters T-shirts shouting at her, while Pandora lurked in the shadows of her mind.

And then there was the argument with Billy.

The clock on the wall said it was eleven in the morning, but she glanced from it and stared at her phone. She'd expected him to text her, but the mobile had stayed quiet all night. She was about to reach for it when her mother entered the room.

'Mum!' she shouted. 'Knock before you come in.'

Gemma Finn sat on the bed and smiled at her daughter. 'It's unlike you not to eat in the morning. Your dad has even made your favourite banana pancakes.'

'I know. I could smell them cooking downstairs.'

'Are you ill, love?'

Ella shook her head. 'I think the sun took it out of me yesterday.'

Her mother touched Ella's forehead. 'Are you sure it's not a reaction from the police visit?'

She twisted her face out of her mother's touch. 'No, it's nothing to do with that.'

Gemma Finn peered at her daughter. 'Your father told me about the conversation you had at the allotment. Are you worried about something?'

'Don't be daft, Mum.' She was worried about many things, none of which she could talk to her parents about.

'So it's nothing to do with Billy?'

Ella slipped out of bed and away from her mother. She glanced at her reflection in the mirror, noticing how her long dark hair looked like a bird's nest after someone had dropped a bomb in it. And the shadows under her eyes belonged to somebody at least thirty years older than her.

'We argued, that's all.'

Damn! Why did I tell her that?

Gemma got off the bed. 'Why did you argue?' She placed a hand on her daughter's arm. 'Is he trying to make you do things you don't want to?'

'Mum!' Ella shouted loud enough to shake the blinds. 'Don't be so daft.'

Ella's mother crossed her arms and looked as upset as she'd ever seen her.

'Well, you're obviously worried about something. You can't hide that from me. And if it wasn't because of the police visit, I can only think it's to do with what your father said about your conversation at the allotment.'

Ella controlled her breathing before she exploded. 'You're right, Mum, it was about the coppers grilling me yesterday.' She had to make the lie convincing enough her mother would stop going on about Billy. 'I told Billy about it, and he said he was worried about me, so I lost my temper and shouted at him. I don't need him to look after me.'

Gemma rubbed along her daughter's arm. 'He's only concerned about you, love, just like me and your dad are. Billy's a good lad. I know he wouldn't do anything to hurt you.'

She hugged her mother, wondering when she'd stop lying to her.

'We'll be okay, Mum. I'll text him later.'

Gemma Finn let go of her daughter and stared around the bedroom.

'At least your room is clean for once, apart from these.'

She reached down to where Ella had dumped her trousers last night.

'No,' Ella shouted as she tried to stop her.

But it was too late.

Gemma grabbed the trousers so they were upside down. That's when the packet of cigarettes tumbled to the floor.

'What's this?' she said as she grabbed them.

'It's not what you think, Mum.'

'What's not what she thinks?' Andrew Finn said as he stepped into the room.

Ella watched his eyes bulge when he saw what his wife held in her hand.

'Oh, Ella,' Gemma said. 'I thought you were better than this.'

The bed creaked under Ella as she sat on it and sighed.

'They're not mine; they're Billy's. I took them from him, and that's why we argued.'

Andrew Finn took the packet. 'Is this why you were in a rush to meet him yesterday?'

Ella peered into both their faces, saddened at seeing the disappointment in them.

'No, I told you. I didn't want him smoking. I meant to throw them in the bin on the way home, but I forgot.'

For once, she was telling them the truth, but she guessed they didn't believe her.

Her parents looked at each other before turning back to Ella. Then her mother spoke.

'So, you lied to me earlier when you said you'd argued about yesterday's police visit?'

Ella knew that, no matter what she said, she couldn't win this time.

'Yes. I didn't want you to know about his cigarettes.'

Her mother's face seemed to have aged ten years in five seconds. 'What else are you doing with him? Are you drinking? Taking drugs?' She glanced at her husband. 'Other things?'

Ella pulled at her hair. 'No, Mum, I told you. There's nothing like that going on. I took the packet from Billy to stop him smoking.'

'You didn't trust him with the cigarettes?' her father said.

Ella's heart sank. 'Yes.'

Gemma Finn appeared to forget what she'd said about Billy not so long ago.

'I don't want you seeing that boy for a while, do you understand?'

Ella accepted that was the best she was going to get and nodded. 'Yes, Mum.'

Her parents stood there in silence and she thought they'd give her some other punishment.

What if they don't believe me and search the room for more cigarettes? They might find the Book of All Life.

'Do you want a late breakfast?' her father said.

Ella jumped from the bed. 'That would be great, Dad. Thanks.'

She followed them downstairs and into the kitchen. Her mother squashed the cigarette packet in her hands and put it into one of the recycling bins. Then Andrew Finn served pancakes for all of them. Ella enjoyed the taste of bananas slipping down her throat while wondering what to say.

Her phone was on the table when it flicked into life with a notification. She was too busy stuffing her face with bits of pancake to stop her mother from grabbing the mobile.

Crap! I hope it's Billy sending me a message, but Mum will probably go ballistic if it is.

'Why is there a picture of Medusa winking on here?'

Toffee sauce dripped from Ella's lips as she sighed with relief. Then she took the phone and read the notification.

'It's a Friend Request on MythMaker.'

'What's MythMaker?' her dad said.

Ella accepted the request without checking the details. 'It's a new game where you can be a mythical creature going on quests and fighting battles.'

She put the mobile in her pocket and continued with her breakfast.

Her mother laughed as she removed empty plates from the table.

'Don't let Detective Inspector Wexford find out about it. He might add it to his terrorist conspiracy theory.'

Ella watched her parents laugh together, glad the drama with the cigarettes and Billy appeared to be over. But she was still concerned about them. They had no memory of Pandora abducting them and no knowledge of Elementals, Light, the Book of All Life, or Ella's adventures in this world and the multiverse.

But I'll have to tell them sometime. Tell them I lied and manipulated them both.

That thought was possessing her mind when her phone vibrated again with another notification. She took it from her pocket, hiding her smile when she saw a text from Billy.

'You'll have to show me how the app works, Ella. It will give me something to do when I'm at the allotment.'

'Sure, Dad. Maybe when I come back later.'

Her mother put two plates into the sink. 'Where are you going?'

She stared at her mother and prepared another lie, but only half of one this time.

'I'm going to ride up to the cliffs and see what the ships look like today.'

'Are you going past the Twist house?' Andrew Finn said.

Ella knew it was a trick question because that was the only way up there with a bike.

'Yes. Do you want me to check to see if it's okay? Make sure nobody has broken in?'

Just like I did last year when I crawled into the kitchen through the window. It's weird to think how much has changed since then.

'No, you're all right, love. But you can see if there's a *For Sale* sign outside of it. I wouldn't put anything past Alan Twist where that house is concerned.'

Gemma Finn placed a hand on her husband's shoulder. 'Perhaps it's time we got a solicitor for this, Andrew. Something must be happening for the police to come here and mention it yesterday.'

He touched his wife's fingers. 'Perhaps.' He glanced at Ella as she got up from the table. 'It's only been a year since your sister and her family disappeared. I don't think he can declare them dead yet.'

Ella wasn't shocked at her father's words, only surprised he'd said them in front of her. Maybe all this fuss with the cigarettes would make them stop treating her like a little kid anymore.

If they knew what I'd been through the last eighteen months, they wouldn't think like that ever again. And I'll be fourteen in less than a week.

But they'd probably both have heart attacks. Something she was desperate to prevent.

Her phone pinged again as she smiled at them. 'I'll let you know if there's a sign up.'

'Make sure you're back before six,' her mother shouted as Ella went to get changed.

She checked the messages as soon as she closed the door behind her: both were from Billy.

I'm sorry about yesterday. Do you forgive me?
And.
It's not as hot today, but I'll buy you an ice cream.
She sent a quick reply.
I'll meet you on the cliffs in forty-five minutes. You know where.

He sent her an emoji of a unicorn. Ella grinned at it before throwing her pyjamas on to the floor. Then she stepped into the shower and let the warm water wake her up.

———

FORTY MINUTES LATER, she'd cycled up the bank out of Saltburn and turned into the path leading up to the cottages on the cliffs. She pedalled slowly as she approached her aunt's house and the barn where they'd put her when she'd lived with them.

There was no *For Sale* sign outside the building, but she didn't care. She rode up to the front door, her face one massive smile when she saw Billy standing there. Ella squeezed the brakes and got off the bike. She thought about running up and hugging him until she realised that would be weird.

Instead, she pushed the bike against the wall near his, still smiling as she went to him.

His grin warmed her heart. 'I'm sorry about what I said. It was cruel, and I didn't mean any of it.'

Ella shook her head. 'I've forgotten about it already. But I can't give you your ciggies back.' She told him how her mother had found them in her bedroom.

'Blimey. What did they do?'

'They said I couldn't see you for a bit.'

Billy laughed. 'Well, that didn't last long.'

She laughed with him. 'What happened with your cousin?'

'Hannah? She thinks she must have lost the packet on the bus from Leeds. She's brilliant, is cousin Hannah, some kind of computer whizz kid, but she hasn't got bags of common sense in her noggin.'

Ella's ribs hurt with all the laughter, and she could hardly believe they'd had that argument only yesterday.

'Are you coming inside with me?'

Billy nodded. 'Wild flying horses couldn't keep me out, my friend.'

'Be careful what you wish for,' Ella said as she led him to the back of the house.

'What if someone's been in and locked it?' Billy whispered to Ella as she climbed on the barrel under the window.

She steadied herself and turned to him. 'Why are you whispering? There's only us here.'

He scratched the top of his head. 'Sorry. I've never broken into a house before.'

Ella placed one hand on the window and lifted it. 'Don't worry. You'll soon get the hang of it.'

She climbed through the gap and into the sink, thankful it wasn't full of dirty water and plates like the last time she'd done this. Ella jumped to the floor as Billy followed her through and sat on the edge.

'It stinks in here.'

'Close the window,' she said. 'We don't want anybody to see it open.'

He did that and climbed down. 'I don't think anyone comes up here anymore, Ella, you know, after all the Twists vanished from the house.'

She peered at the layers of dust everywhere, pushing

back the bad memories of the six months with her aunt and her family.

'What do you mean?'

Billy frowned. 'People believe this place is jinxed now, or haunted.'

Ella laughed. 'Ghosts don't exist.'

She went to leave the kitchen, but he put his hand on her arm.

'Are you sure? With all the strange stuff we saw last year - dragons, witches, unicorns and all the rest, plus what you encountered in the multiverse - how can you be sure ghosts aren't real as well as those other things?'

Ella couldn't, but she doubted it.

'Do you believe in life after death, Billy?'

He shrugged. 'I don't know. Do you?'

'Whatever strange things we've seen and are yet to see, I doubt this house is haunted. So come on.'

She stepped out of the kitchen and into the corridor.

'What are we looking for?' Billy said.

Ella peered at the framed photos on the wall of her missing cousins, aunt, and uncle.

'The Twists must have gone somewhere after Pandora left here. When I got back from the multiverse, the police closed this house off, and I've never had the chance to search it.'

'What makes you think you'll find something if they couldn't?'

She knew he didn't intend to make it sound like a criticism, but it still came out like that.

'I might have no Light left in me, but if there's a clue to what happened to the Twists in here, I'm more likely to see it than the police.'

'Because of your connection to Elementals?'

Ella nodded. 'Yes. You remember what Pandora did to Dolly, Dotty and Daisy, don't you?'

Billy grimaced. 'I still have nightmares about it, the way she squeezed those three girls into one giant misshapen body.'

'And because Pandora did that using her Light, the Light I eventually took from her, I believe there must be a connection between my cousins and me. So even if they're not in the house, there could be a trail to them only I can see or find.'

'Okay, I guess that makes sense. Should we split up to make it quicker?'

Ella grinned at him. 'I thought you were scared you'd bump into some ghosts?'

'No, no, I was only joking about that.'

She put a hand on his arm, feeling it tremble under his jumper.

'We'll stick together. I have to see all of the house anyway, so you might as well be with me.'

He seemed happy with that. 'Okay. Where do we start?'

'Downstairs. We've done the kitchen, so there's only the living room and dining room to search.'

They went into the dining room first. Ella tried not to think of all the times she'd sat in there with her cousins as they made snide remarks at her, and Daisy kicked at her under the table. It was empty now, save for a faded yellow cover over it. Dead flies lay on the floor as if dropped there to form a macabre dot-to-dot diagram.

Billy grimaced as he dodged the unmoving insects. 'Shall we check the drawers and cupboards?'

Ella thought about it for a second. 'No. It's more about if I can see something like the doorway I went through to enter the multiverse.'

'Do you think that's what happened to them, that they got sucked into another world?'

She ran her fingers through the dust on the table. 'They have to be somewhere, don't they?' She turned to Billy. 'The mystery house only I could see wasn't on the cliffs anymore when I returned from the multiverse. If that disappeared when Pandora left Earth, maybe the thing she created from my cousins did as well.'

'But what about your aunt and uncle?'

Ella shrugged. 'My mother thinks Ida skipped town, ran away when she thought her sister was coming here. Perhaps she did and took the girls with her.'

Billy picked up a book from the dresser, and Ella saw it was a Bible.

I don't remember that being here.

'That thing Pandora made of your cousins. People would have seen that, no matter where your aunt took them.'

'Which makes it more likely they're not in this world anymore.' She glanced around. 'And there could be a doorway in this place somewhere.'

'One only you can see?'

'Yes, like the mystery house on the cliffs where I found the Book of All Life.'

Billy put the Bible back. 'And where all of this started.'

Ella didn't reply, leaving the dining room and moving into the living room. She stopped inside the doorway, peering at the large flat screen TV, the bookcases empty of books, a coffee table, and the three-piece suite. She'd spent little time in there after the police had brought her north from London since her uncle, who wasn't her uncle, had set up living arrangements for her in the barn.

She hadn't minded staying in there. It was cold at night,

but it kept her away from her cousins, and that's where she'd met Ratter.

Poor Ratter. I wonder if the Elemental who took over her little body put a strain on her heart.

She tried to forget about her animal friend who'd died while she was in the multiverse and remembered who else had been in that barn with her: the horses.

What happened to the horses when the Twists disappeared?

'There's no doorway to another world in here, is there, Ella?'

'No,' she said. 'Let's check upstairs.'

They searched through the three bedrooms and the bathroom, but found nothing unusual. She was thinking it had been a daft idea to go into the house when Billy pointed above her.

'There's an attic up there.'

She looked up, seeing the entrance and the hook to pull it down.

'I didn't even know that was there.'

'Hang on,' Billy said. He disappeared into one bedroom and returned with a chair. 'We'll need this to get inside.' He placed it under the attic.

Ella put a hand on it. 'Shall I go first?'

Billy grinned at her. 'Me ma says I'm no gentleman, but I'll prove her wrong now.'

He got onto the chair and stretched up to reach for the handle. Then he pulled on it. Dust fell from the ceiling. Ella waved her hands in the air to stop it from getting into her hair and on her face, but failed. She sneezed and coughed.

'Watch what you're doing, Billy.'

'Sorry. This is stronger than it looks.' He twisted his neck to smile at her. 'But, so am I.'

He gave it another hard yank and the entrance fell open. Before she could tell him to be careful, he'd stuck his head inside, then climbed into the attic.

'What can you see?' she shouted.

But only silence came back.

Ella stood with one hand on the chair, the other curling into a fist as she remembered how she'd dug into her flesh at the allotment yesterday.

'Billy, are you okay?'

The hairs on her arms sprang up and her legs trembled. She was putting one leg on the chair as Billy stuck his head out of the attic.

'It was pitch black when I got up here. I couldn't see anything and tripped over a box of old toys. Ma won't be happy I've scuffed me kecks, but at least I found the light switch.' He beamed at her. 'Are you coming up?'

He held a hand down to her. Ella stepped onto the chair and took it, feeling the damp in his fingers. Billy helped her into the attic and she scrutinised the place, which was as big as the living room. It was cleaner than she'd expected, with only a film of dust covering most things. A skylight in the roof let a small amount of light in to dance between the beams and meet in several arches. An old table stood in the corner, with boxes of toys dotted everywhere.

Ella reached into one of them, finding tattered games of *Monopoly*, *Cluedo* and *Connect 4*. She lifted the *Monopoly* box and the top slid open. Fake money spilt onto the floor, followed by the pieces she was familiar with from when she'd played the game with her parents in London: the top hat, the boot, a battleship, racing car, and her favourite, the Scottie dog.

She picked up the dog, feeling the metal between her fingers, wondering if she'd ever get back to those innocent times again with her mum and dad.

'Watch out for *Jumanji*,' Billy said.

'What?' she replied.

He grinned at her. 'You know, the game that sucks you into another world of danger and monsters.'

'It's too late for that,' Ella said.

'This is weird,' he said.

Ella dropped the Scottie dog into the box and went to Billy, who was staring at a shelf full of globes with small figurines inside them.

'I think they're clockwork figures,' Ella said. 'My mum gave me one when I was a kid. It had Mickey Mouse in it.'

'Yeah,' he said. 'I know what they are. But look at what's inside these.'

She moved closer to him and saw what he meant: there were eight domes on the shelf, but none of them had Disney figures or cartoon characters inside. The nearest one to her appeared to have a miniature plastic version of Aunt Ida in it. The one next to it contained a figurine of Uncle George. Then there were tiny replicas of her cousins, Dolly, Dotty and Daisy.

Billy clutched at his chest. 'Do you think... do you think this is what happened to them?'

Ella calmed her thumping heart. 'No, that's silly. Maybe they had these made for presents or something.'

She was going to grab one when he stopped her. 'What about the others?'

Ella turned her face from the figurines of the Twists and saw what was in the other domes: miniature replicas of her, Billy and Dora.

Dora, who was Pandora.

Her hand froze in the air, the breath creeping out of her. Then the temperature dropped and a chill breeze invaded the attic. She was about to say something when she noticed movement in all the ornaments.

'They're alive,' Billy shouted.

Ella froze, her legs like ice blocks. She couldn't take her eyes off the domes as, one by one, they cracked and the tiny figurines climbed out of them.

The one that looked like her oldest cousin, Dolly, pointed at her and spoke.

But she was so small, Ella didn't hear what she said.

Ella's arms finally moved as they trembled. 'What?'

This time, the voice was as loud as a roaring hurricane.

'You did this to us!' the miniature Dolly screamed.

Before Ella could do anything, all the tiny Twists jumped at her.

7 UNHAPPY BIRTHDAY

Ella stumbled back, her legs bumping into a table as she fell. A sharp stab of electricity ran up her spine, turning into a hammer that smashed into the rear of her skull as she lay on the floor. Her eyes blurred, but she knew what she saw crawling over her chest towards her face was real: tiny figurines of her cousins, Dolly, Dotty, and Daisy, digging their little plastic fingers into her shirt and dragging themselves closer to her head. She felt them moving over her skin, and every part of her shivered.

Their eyes bulged red and yellow as they shouted at her together.

'You did this, Smella. You did this, you did this, you did this.'

They kept crawling over her, chanting those same words until they were burnt into her brain. Once, a long time ago, she'd fallen in the garden into a nest of spiders. Her mother had pulled her up, but not before some spiders had crawled over her hands and arms. She'd been too young to realise they wouldn't harm her, so her body had spasmed with terror as her mother cleared the spiders from her trembling flesh.

Now she felt like that again.

Ella's back ached as if she was carrying a horse on it, but the pain was enough to spur her into action. She swung her arm across her chest and sent the murderous tiny Twists flying over the attic.

She was rolling over to get up, when she froze at the sight next to her: the *Monopoly* figurines charged towards her, their metallic grey forms now transformed into fiery blood-red shapes. The Scottie dog was at the front, grown to the size of Ella's hand, with its teeth sharpened and ready to bite. Behind it, the other pieces were all twisted and deformed, with only one thing in common to all of their new shapes: the monstrous carnivorous fangs champing at the bit to get to her.

Ella dug her fingers into the floorboards as the maniac *Monopoly* figures hurled themselves at her like a great sandstorm.

She thrust out her arm to repel them, but they never arrived.

When she looked up, Billy was standing over her with a brush shaking in his hands.

Then he dragged her up. 'We have to get out of here.'

She didn't argue, catching her breath as she watched the dome figurines and the *Monopoly* shapes gathering for another attack. Beyond them, the floor moved and shimmered as if a great worm was ready to pounce from underneath the floorboards.

'Come on,' she said as she dragged Billy with her to the exit.

Ella didn't look back, but she heard the voices again.

'You did this, Smella. You did this, you did this, you did this.'

She pushed Billy in front of her, fighting against her nerves as he scrambled out of the attic. Ella was moving to follow him when something grabbed her foot.

Then it pulled her back and threw her against the wall.

Ella bounced off the concrete, falling and expecting the tiny demonic creatures to swarm over her again.

But they didn't.

She looked up to see a creature crawling through the dirt towards her. Its body was all out of shape, the legs and arms twisted and pointing in directions they shouldn't have been. The head was at the wrong angle, jutting out from the neck like that bent tower in Italy. The flesh on the face was mottled and moved as if it was quicksand. One eye was bigger than the other, pulsating red and yellow like a poisonous fried egg. It was a dreadful sight from Ella's worst nightmares, but she recognised who it was.

Dolly.

'I missed my birthday party because of you, Smella.'

Her voice was like nails dragged over broken glass. And then other voices came from behind her.

'We all missed our birthdays because of you, Smella.'

Ella didn't want to take her gaze away from Dolly, but she couldn't help herself, glancing around to peer at the wall.

And her other cousins peered back at her, Daisy and Dotty, their heads melting out of the concrete and reaching for her. They weren't as monstrous as Dolly, but their tongues wriggled towards her as if they were snakes, while their eyes were nothing but darkness.

Then their arms burst from the concrete and grabbed hold of her.

Ella tried to squirm out of their grasp, but it was impossible. Instead, she turned her head to the thing crawling closer to her.

'Where are our presents, cousin?' the creature looking like Dolly said.

It smelt of dirt and dead vegetables, of burning flesh. And when it spoke, it sounded like the death cries from every abattoir in the world.

'You should sing us a happy birthday song since we haven't seen you for so long.'

Nails dug into Ella's back as she wriggled in their grasp.

'Where's your mother, Dolly? Where's Ida?'

The thing stopped moving towards her, and she felt the hands relaxing on her arms.

'She's dead,' the three of them said together. 'Our mother sings to us from her grave.'

Ella gazed at the creature, convinced now it wasn't her cousin.

But how can I be sure?

'Does she have a grave?' Ella said.

'Of course,' the thing in front of her said. 'I dug it myself. She tried to climb out of it, but we pushed her back in, her three loving daughters.'

Ella felt the grip on her release. 'Why would you do that if you all loved her?'

The creature rose and sat cross-legged before her.

'I don't know. Why would we do that?'

With her body free, Ella forced her back into the wall and placed her hands flat on the floorboards. Then a sound came from the side of her like the pop of a burst balloon. She tried not to look at the things which slid past her, but it was impossible: two smaller versions of the creature that wasn't Dolly crawled over the floor like wet snails leaving a terrible trail behind them. The air stank of the dead as they joined their sister to stare at Ella through torturously deformed faces.

Ella took a deep breath. 'You wouldn't do that because you're not my cousins.'

The creatures looked at each other, and even in those misshapen eyes, she recognised their fear. They raised their gnarled hands to their heads and spoke as one.

'What... what are we?'

'Do you remember Pandora?' Ella said.

'No,' they replied together.

Just as I thought.

'Pandora came here and did bad things, dreadful things. She hurt my cousins, used her power to change them into something terrible. But, somehow, I don't know how, she left a memory of that here. And that memory lingered and festered for twelve months. It might never have reawakened if I hadn't returned to the house, but I did and triggered it into life. And that terrible memory transformed into you. What happened next, with the figurines and you, was only a reaction to me being here. You couldn't help yourself.'

She stood and wiped the dust from her clothes.

'What will happen to us now?' the thing that wasn't Dolly said.

Ella looked over the attic, seeing the figurines and *Monopoly* shapes lying unmoving.

'I think you'll disappear when I leave.'

The creatures stared at her through tear-filled eyes. 'We'll die?'

Ella moved towards the exit. 'All bad memories should die; otherwise, how can anyone move forward with their lives?'

She turned from them as they faded, glancing at the floor below her.

And saw Billy unconscious on the carpet.

'Billy!' she shouted as she scrambled down. Ella jumped off the chair and knelt next to him, putting one hand under his neck.

Then his eyes flickered open. 'I'll never smoke cigarettes again, I promise.'

Relief flooded out of her. 'What happened to you?'

He sat up and rubbed at the back of his neck. 'I slipped when I landed on the chair. The next thing I remember is feeling this bump on me noggin and you trying to kiss me.'

She jerked away from him. 'I did not, Billy Pudding.'

He grinned at her. 'Relax, Ella. I'm only messing with ya.' He glanced up at the attic. 'What happened to you up there?'

Ella dragged him up. 'I'll tell you when we get outside.'

'You don't want to keep searching for this magic portal?'

She shook her head. 'No. I've had enough of this house to last me a lifetime. We'll have to find my cousins some other way.'

But I'm convinced they're still alive now.

He didn't argue, following her downstairs and back to the kitchen. Then they climbed out of the window and she closed it again. They stood next to their bikes while Ella told him everything that had happened while he was unconscious.

Billy kept rubbing at his bruise. 'Blimey. I hope I never have bad memories like that.' He glanced at the barn. 'Do you want to check in there as well?'

Ella gazed at the place where she'd lived for six months and wondered what memories would linger in there. Hers were all good, but other things had happened in there:

under Pandora's orders, Harpies had attacked her and Billy. And a teenage Irish boy had killed a dragon to save them. Plus, Pandora had used her Light to twist three girls into one monstrous thing.

No, there was no need to enter that barn.

Ella shook her head. 'Probably best to go home and start again tomorrow.'

She removed the phone from her pocket, surprised she'd had no message from her parents. There were half a dozen notifications from the MythMaker app, but she ignored them. Then, as she moved towards her bike, she heard Billy's mobile ping.

He took it out and stared at it. 'Wow!'

'Are you getting loads of notifications from that game as well?'

Billy placed a finger on the screen, and she guessed he was flicking through pages.

'No. I had too many of those, so I turned them off. This is from the DAM website.'

Ella narrowed her eyes at him. 'What? Why would you have notifications set for the Destroy All Monsters site?'

He stepped closer to her. 'They have updates of sightings of their so-called monsters for all over the country. I set a notification for if they posted any local to us. So go to the site and see what they've just added.'

She bit the top of her lip and did what he said. The DAM home page was full of propaganda and paranoia, the coordinators hating on anything different to them and crying out for a call to arms: not from the police or the army, but for the British people to "stand up for your country and fight against the monsters."

Ella ignored the section where DAM listed what they

thought were monsters and checked the Twitter feed, which had their latest rants. She read out the first one.

'Sighting of a giant ghoul in Saltburn today. Eyewitnesses say they saw the monster near the viaduct. Check out the photo.'

She clicked on the image to get a bigger version, peering into the screen to see a blurry photo of what could have been a Bigfoot. Ella knew of it from TV shows she'd seen, how it was also called a Sasquatch in Canadian and American folklore. It was an ape-like creature purported to inhabit the forests of North America. She guessed if it was an Elemental, it could have crossed over to Earth there.

'It's probably a fake, Billy. But even if it's real, it's getting too late to check it out today.' It was nearly five o'clock, and she knew she had to be home by six if she didn't want to upset her parents again. 'We can go tomorrow.'

'Take a closer look at the face, Ella.'

She sighed and did that, pushing her head into the screen until it buzzed against her skin.

And that's when she saw what he meant.

The Bigfoot looked like Dolly.

8 SMOKE ON THE WATER

Ella's hand shook as she stared at the figure that might be one of her missing cousins.

'We need to go there now, Billy, to the viaduct.'

'I thought you had to go home?'

She looked at the time on her phone before putting the mobile into her pocket. Her parents had told her to be back by six, and that was only an hour away.

'I'll text my mum and dad and tell them...'

What would she tell them? They'd told her not to see Billy anymore, so she couldn't say she was at his house. And they knew she didn't have any other friends here.

'They could be wrong, these DAM people, Ella. The photo might be a fake. There are loads of those on the internet. Only yesterday, I saw one of a UFO in London which was clearly not real.'

She grabbed her bike and got on it. 'You don't have to come with me. I'll understand.' Ella glanced over her shoulder at the Twist house. 'What happened in there was scary for both of us.'

He pulled up his bike next to hers and stuck out his chest. 'I wasn't scared, and I'm coming with you.'

She smiled at him as they rode off and down the bank. The oppressive heat had disappeared as the wind caressed her face. She went first as they cycled along the pavement and off the road, smelling the sea drifting in the surrounding air. She kept a tight hold of the brakes as they went around a bend and came out at the bottom. The ocean was in front of them, but they turned away and stopped outside the Valley Gardens.

'It will be quicker going through here,' Ella said.

He rubbed at the back of his skull, and she wondered how nasty his bruise was.

'We'll still have to go up once we get to the coffee shop in the middle.'

'Maybe we should postpone this, Billy, and take you to the hospital.'

He pulled his fingers from his head. 'What? Why would we do that?'

She reached out her hand, thinking she'd put it on his arm, but changing her mind at the last minute and placing it on his bike.

'That was a nasty fall you had in the house. You could have a delayed concussion or maybe some internal bleeding.'

He laughed at her. 'You've been watching too many medical shows. There's nothing wrong with me.'

Ella peered into his eyes, staring deep to make sure he was okay.

'Fine. If we ride as fast as we can, we might have enough time to have a good look around for this Bigfoot, and I'll get back home without being too late. Do you remember where the sighting was?'

She'd walked under the viaduct once with her parents. Scaffolding had covered it; it had been undergoing some well-needed repairs, from what she remembered.

'It was somewhere near the beck, according to the website.'

Ella peered into the Valley Gardens, knowing they'd have to be careful on their bikes because of the people in there with their kids or walking their dogs.

It's going to be a close call for me to be home for six.

Then she had a brainwave.

I'll text them at ten to six and say I've got a puncture and a flat tyre.

She grinned at Billy. 'Okay. Let's get a move on, Pudding.'

Ella went before him, pedalling slowly to dodge the people in their way. It took two minutes to hit the first incline, a narrow path up past the café. It was closed, so nobody was there as she changed gears on her bike and steeled her legs to cycle up.

The first time she'd made this journey, Ella had breathed a sigh of relief after getting up the incline until she turned the corner and realised there were a lot more steep climbs, and they twisted and curved like a plate of spaghetti.

But she was prepared now and paced herself going up. That was until Billy inched past and got in front of her in between the trees.

'I told you I was faster,' he shouted as he disappeared around a curve and out of sight.

Ella took a deep breath and lifted out of her seat, rising above it as she increased the speed of her legs pumping on the pedals. When she turned the corner, she saw Billy's back and smiled because she knew she'd catch him soon.

And I'll get there before him.

She dodged a few dog walkers coming in the opposite direction and sat on his bike wheel, imagining she was a rider at the Tour de France and she'd have that yellow jersey before Billy.

It was early evening and the air was cooler, which was a good thing considering the effort she was putting into the ride. It was tough going, but she enjoyed it, glad to have something else to focus on rather than what they'd gone through in the Twist house. She'd doubted Billy earlier when he'd said ghosts might be real, but after what happened with those things that thought they were her cousins, she wasn't so sure.

Maybe that's what ghosts or spirits really are, just bad memories lingering around houses and other places. They could be a form of Light, all twisted and dark, that can't leave the place where something terrible happened.

When Ella had travelled through the multiverse, every living thing she'd met had had their own name for what Pandora called the Light. So now, when she thought about it, she could see why ghosts could be a corrupt version of Light, using bad memories to create a physical presence.

Ella continued behind Billy as they finished the climb, getting ready for the next descent. She kept thinking about her theory of what ghosts might be, hoping one day she'd be able to talk to her parents about all of this. They were both scientists, so they'd know more about different types of energy than she did.

As that thought stuck in her head, she caught Billy, seeing him squeeze his brakes as they came to the trickiest part of the downhill: not only was it steep, but the path wasn't flat and was covered in little stones.

But those things didn't bother her.

She let go of her brakes and sped past him, grinning as

she did. As she used her hands and legs to manoeuvre around the corners, she saw the viaduct looming ahead. Metal and plastic hung from most of the stone, and she guessed the repairs were still ongoing.

The wind blew through her hair, and at that precise moment, she forgot she was anything but an ordinary teenage girl. There were no worries about missing cousins, or monsters, or Elementals, or Pandora, or about how she'd deceived her parents. Instead, blood pumped through her veins like electricity flowing from a socket and into a kettle. She felt it warming her, sensing she was on the verge of something important. Ella's heart thumped against her ribs, sending a rhythm through her body which transformed into music as she stopped pedalling and let the wheels go of their own accord.

Somewhere in her head, Ella could hear people singing along to *Dancing Queen*, and it was as if none of the last eighteen months had happened to her. The tyres skidded over the path, with the little stones bouncing off the rubber. As her senses were overwhelmed with many sensations, she wished her life could be like this forever.

And then that thought vanished as she slammed on the brakes before the bike crashed through the field in front of the viaduct.

She grinned at the magnificent example of Victorian architecture as Billy pulled up next to her.

'I guess you're faster than me after all,' he said as he wiped the sweat from his cheek.

Ella removed the phone from her pocket and checked the time. Then she told him about her plan and the flat tyre.

'So make sure I don't forget to text them in thirty minutes.'

Billy put a hand to his head and gave her a mock salute. 'Aye, aye, captain.'

She scanned the area, remembering how far they were from the beck under the viaduct.

'Okay. We can ride a bit more before we have to get off the bikes and push them down to the water.'

He nodded at her. 'Shall I check the DAM website to see if there have been any more sightings of the Bigfoot?'

'Yes,' Ella said. 'And let's hope there aren't too many people here.'

The last time she'd been here, which was only a few months ago, there were kids messing about in the water. If there was a creature there who was her cousin, she didn't want anybody around who might get hurt.

Thoughts of dangerous Elementals occupied her as Billy finished on his phone.

'There's nothing new on the DAM website about the Bigfoot. I don't think most of them care about what goes on around here, more concerned about all the London monsters.'

Ella looked at him. 'London monsters?'

'Yeah. There have been loads of reports there of strange creatures attacking people. So I guess they might be panicking a bit.'

Ella tried not to think of that because she still had a friend in London, Lara Crowley.

I'll have to go back to see her when this is over.

'Come on. Let's get to the beck.'

They cycled a little more before getting off the bikes and pushing them under the viaduct. She looked up at it as they went, trying to remember the last time she was on a train. The shadow of the structure settled over her, cooling her skin as they headed to the water. Ella was glad they were the only ones there, but there was no guarantee that would last long.

Billy strode next to her as they reached the beck and lay their bikes on to the ground.

'What do we do now?'

She didn't have an answer, so went by instinct.

Ella lifted her head and shouted, 'Dolly, are you here?'

Her voice was so loud, disturbing a few birds from the surrounding trees.

'Are you sure this is a good idea?' Billy said.

She shrugged. 'I've got nothing else. You?'

He shook his head before opening his mouth. 'Dolly, are you here?'

They did that for two minutes, breathing hard and shouting even harder.

Apart from troubling the birds, they got no response.

'I guess it was a long shot,' he said. 'At least you won't have to lie to your parents. If we leave now, you'll make it back for six.'

Ella turned her hands into fists, frustration seeping out of her to match the rhythm of the water flowing through the beck.

Then she had another brainwave.

'Dolly, are you here? I've come for your birthday. I've got your present with me.'

Silence surrounded them as they stood and waited. Everywhere was calm, the only sound the slow beating of their hearts.

So Ella sang.

'Happy birthday to you, happy birthday to you, happy birthday dear Dolly, happy birthday to you.'

As she finished singing and her heart thumped with an

all too familiar ache, a new noise broke the silence under the viaduct.

Across the water, the sound of broken branches stretched out to Ella. As she looked over, the Bigfoot strode towards her.

Only it wasn't Bigfoot.

It was her cousin, Dolly.

9 UNDER THE BRIDGE

Billy gasped as Dolly Twist stomped into the beck. The water covered her ankles as she peered at them.

Ella moved back, gazing at her cousin. Dolly appeared ordinary enough: she wasn't part of the combined creature Pandora had created in the barn last year. She also looked nothing like the deformed thing Ella had encountered in the Twist house less than an hour ago. Instead, her clothes seemed clean and her face appeared normal.

'Dolly, do you know me? I'm your cousin, Ella. And this is my friend, Billy. Billy Pudding, remember?'

She noticed him grimace when she called him that, telling herself off for being so stupid not to think about his feelings. While she did that, Dolly started swaying in the water and mumbling under her breath.

Billy took out his phone. 'Maybe we should call for an ambulance. She doesn't look well.'

Before Ella could reply, Dolly stumbled forward. She crashed through the beck and fell in front of them.

Ella ran to her. 'Dolly, Dolly, are you okay?'

She lay there, half in and half out of the water. Billy stood next to Ella with the phone in his hand.

And then Dolly leapt up and grabbed the mobile from him.

'Hey,' Billy shouted as he toppled into Ella. The weight of him took them both down into the mud.

Dolly loomed over them, lifting her head to glare at Ella.

'I remember you, Smella. You hurt me. You hurt all of us.'

She threw the phone into the beck. It splashed into the water and sank. Ella dug her fingers into the dirt. This was no bad memory returning to attack her this time.

'What happened to you, Dolly?'

Dolly glared at her through bloodshot eyes. Then she lifted her hands before bringing them crashing into the sides of her head. She did that for thirty seconds before jerking her neck to stare into the sky. Then she let out a long, spine-tingling howl like a wolf baying at the moon.

Ella moved back through the dirt like a crab, dragging Billy with her.

'She's lost her mind,' he whispered.

Ella pulled him up. 'Maybe, maybe not.'

She felt the tension in Billy's arms, recognising his desperation to flee. But she wouldn't leave her cousin again, no matter how much she knew Dolly hated her.

Ella stood there and waited for the calm to return to Dolly. When it did, she glared at Ella.

'I don't know what happened to my sisters or me.' She glanced into the sky before snapping her gaze back to Ella. 'We were in the barn. I remember that and fighting the harpies before the dragon and the witch burst inside.'

'Do you remember Pandora?'

Dolly's legs trembled as she moved forward. 'Yes, she

was your little friend Dora.' She held her hands up and peered into her palms. 'But she did something to us, to me and Dotty and Daisy.' She dropped her arms to her sides. 'What did she do to us?'

Ella stepped towards her cousin.

'She changed you, Dolly, transformed all three of you into something different.' Ella was close to Dolly, so close she could smell the sweat and dirt on her cousin. 'But you're normal now.'

Dolly puffed out her cheeks and stared at Ella. 'I'll never be normal again, Smella, and it's all your fault.'

She threw herself at Ella and knocked her to the ground. They rolled through the filth, with Dolly clutching at Ella's face and hair. She was smaller than Dolly, but not by much. She'd grown since she'd last seen her cousin, and she was stronger in both mind and body.

Ella got her knee up and into Dolly's belly, getting enough leverage to push her cousin off her. She shoved Dolly back, so she crashed into the beck. Then Ella turned to make sure Billy was okay.

But he wasn't there.

When she heard the splashing in the water, she turned and saw him retrieving his phone from the beck.

'You'll have to call the police, Ella. I don't think my mobile is working.'

She shook her head. 'I'm not calling them, Billy. We need to calm Dolly down first and find out what happened to her sisters.'

'We're here, Smella. We've always been here.'

They spoke together as they appeared from the bushes, Daisy and Dotty walking towards their sister. Their arms and legs jerked left and right as they moved through the water as if they were grasping for things only they could see. When they reached Dolly, they picked her up.

Ella stared at them, remembering the last time she'd seen them in the barn before Pandora had squashed them into one person. They were three individuals again, seemingly a group of ordinary teenagers.

But Ella knew that wasn't true.

Whatever Pandora did to them is still inside their heads.

Her instincts told her to get out of there. To run for the bike and leave as quickly as possible. Her cousins had returned, and they weren't her responsibility anymore.

But I can't leave them like this. And where are Aunt Ida and Uncle George?

'Do any of you remember what happened in the barn?' Ella said.

Dolly stepped between her sisters, the mania appearing to have left her for now.

'We were three minds pushed into one, like size eight feet squashed into size five shoes.' She pressed a hand against the side of her skull, and her sisters did the same. 'It was terrible, having all those other thoughts fighting with yours to get control.' Her eyes shrank into her face. 'Three brains were forced into one head, struggling to see who was in charge. There were so many thoughts there, so many things burning through our brain.'

Dotty moved forward. 'But one thought alone possessed us: the desire to kill you, Smella.'

'So we attacked you,' Dolly said. 'And then everything went black, and we woke, still in one body, surrounded by darkness.'

'And the silence,' Daisy said. 'We suffered in silence for an endless time. All we had was the dark and each other.'

'Only that and our hatred of you, Smella,' Dotty said.

'Finally, we appeared here, in these bushes, and what's the first thing we hear?'

'Me, shouting for Dolly,' Ella said.

Dotty laughed like a hyena. 'See, it's fate, Smella. We wanted to kill you then, and we still do.'

Ella stared at her middle cousin, remembering her in a coma in the hospital. Then she'd begged Seraphina, the witch, to save her. So Seraphina did by sticking her fingers into Dotty's skull to manipulate her brain out of that unwanted sleep.

Seraphina said I'd regret her doing that, and she might be proved right at any second. I can't fight three of them if they intend to kill me.

Ella turned to Billy. 'Run. I'll hold them off.'

He shook his head. 'I won't abandon you.'

Dotty stepped out of the water and rubbed her hands.

'That's good. All I did in that dark, terrible silence was dream of killing you both.' She cracked her knuckles as she inched forward. 'They'll be long, torturous deaths, I promise you.'

Ella couldn't move, waiting for one of her cousins to pull Dotty back.

But they didn't.

Instead, they moved for her.

She turned and ran with Billy, sprinting up the mud towards the bridge over the beck. She didn't look back, hoping her cousins were still too confused to catch up with them. The air rushed through her lungs as they sprinted over the dirt, her legs aching as they picked up speed until they reached their bikes.

Should we leave them here? Would it be easier to cycle or run uphill?

Before she could decide, Dotty was on her back.

Ella crashed to the ground, rolling into the filth and seeing Dolly and Daisy pull Billy down so they could get on top of him. They pinned him there as Ella screamed.

'Leave him alone. It's me you want.'

She grappled with Dotty and they tumbled into the fence around the viaduct. They sat facing each other, with hands digging deep into each other's arms.

Dotty sneered at her. 'That's right, cousin, but we'll have some fun with him as well.'

Ella yelled again, but it was inside her head this time. She gripped on to Dotty, regretting letting Seraphina bring her out of that coma.

No, I didn't let her. I asked her. I virtually begged her.

And now that decision was about to get her and Billy killed.

Despair sped through her as she continued to hold on to Dotty.

And then her fingers tingled.

It was like a small jolt of electricity at first, as if she'd touched something full of static and it was jumping into her.

Only she knew it wasn't electricity.

It's Light.

The Light Pandora used to squash the three of them together. So even though they've separated, there must still be a little Light inside them.

And she could use it.

Ella dug her nails into her cousin and focused on the Light, drawing it into her until she felt like a battery ready to explode.

Dotty grinned at her. 'Stick your fingers into me all you want, Smella. I kind of like it.'

Ella smiled back at her. 'Enjoy this, then.' She flexed her hands and her brain at the same time.

Then the Light flew out of her and shot Dotty across the ground.

Ella jumped up and turned to Billy's struggle.

'What did you do?' Dolly said.

'The same thing I'll do to you, cousin, if you don't let him go.'

But she wasn't as confident as she sounded. Ella knew she'd used most of the Light she'd taken from Dotty to knock her away.

Dolly got off Billy. 'You're lying, Smella. I can see it in your face. Whatever you did, you burnt yourself out with poor Dotty.'

She was lurching at Ella, hands outstretched, when a noise stopped her. Ella heard it as well, turning around to see what it was.

'What the...?'

Ella couldn't believe her eyes, staring at a dozen people walking across the field towards them.

Daisy jumped off Billy. 'It's the army.'

Ella peered at them. She wasn't sure if it was the military, but they were all wearing uniforms. And they carried weapons with them.

The closer they got, the more she was convinced the one in front was a woman.

'Take all the girls, but leave the boy,' Ella heard her say. 'We don't need him.'

Ella leapt up and turned to Billy. 'Cover your face.'

He turned back as the uniformed people reached the fence. It was a woman inside the combat suit and mask. Ella was sure of it.

There was a smile behind the visor as the woman aimed her gun at Ella.

That's when Ella closed her eyes.

And let the rest of the Light out of her body in one giant burst.

It exploded out of her, firing out of each pore and muscle. She stood there with her arms out like the brightest clock in the world, her hands pointing at three and nine. Heat radiated out of her in every direction, and she hoped Billy had done as she'd said.

Ella had once tried to take a lightbulb out of the socket while it was still warm, and it had singed her fingers. She felt like that again, only the heat was inside her and it didn't burn; it made her feel alive.

When she opened her eyes, all the uniforms were flat on the floor. Her cousins were also unconscious, but she couldn't do anything about them now. Billy was kneeling with his head between his legs.

She went to him. 'Are you okay?'

He lifted his head and grinned. 'Thanks for the warning.' He stood and pointed at the people. 'What do we do about them?'

'Nothing,' Ella said. 'Let's get our bikes and go home.'

'You've got no argument from me,' Billy said.

Before they left, Ella turned back to the fence and the woman lying there. She was mumbling with her hand outstretched and Ella saw something between her fingers.

She stepped towards the woman and took it: a card with text and numbers on it. She slipped it into her pocket and headed for her bike, glancing at her cousins as she went.

Whoever these uninformed people are, maybe the Twists will be safe with them.

Ella kept saying it as they left.

10 CAT PEOPLE

Ella and Billy didn't look back until they were out of the gardens and into Saltburn. They'd cycled the last part, even though it was a struggle for Ella to get uphill this time. She pushed her legs harder than ever before, her fingers straining on the bike as she expected someone to grab her at any second. When they reached the war memorial, Ella stopped to catch her breath. Only then did she turn around to see if they'd been followed.

But all she saw were adults with kids, and teenagers kicking a football. The sound of the ball bouncing off the wall matched the noises rebounding inside her skull. She gazed at the people playing with their children, wondering if any of them were undercover soldiers stationed there to catch them.

Ella shook the thought from her head and steadied her breathing. Her heart was thumping so hard against her chest, she thought she might crack a rib.

Billy skidded to a halt as he caught up with her. 'Who were those people?'

She nodded at the bandstand ahead of them. 'We'll get some rest there.'

'Aren't you worried they'll come after us?'

His voice shook as he spoke, but Ella didn't reply until she'd got her bike under the bandstand.

'Not with all these people around. I don't know who those soldiers were, but I can't imagine they'd be daft enough to storm up here with their weapons where everyone can see them.'

Billy held his bike as he sat next to her.

'Maybe they're connected to that Destroy All Monsters group, like their military wing or sumthin'.'

Ella scrunched up her cheeks. 'I doubt that. They were too professional. That DAM website looks like a bunch of amateurs runs it.'

As she said that, two blokes strode past them wearing DAM T-shirts, depicting a large human hand strangling a monster. The same illustration was on the rear of their shirts: a huge man with octopus arms stretching out of his back.

Billy nudged up to her and she smelt the sweat dripping off him.

'Look,' he whispered, 'they have spies everywhere.'

Perhaps he's right and we should get out of here.

Ella watched the men walk past them and into the Valley Gardens.

What will we do next?

A large bus pulled up opposite them and a group of tourists got out. She observed them as if in slow motion, a bunch of older folks chatting about how beautiful the place was. A few of them went to the war memorial, while others gazed at the wire sculpture of a family of three outside the bandstand.

'We'll be okay, Billy. Nothing's going to happen to us with all these people here.'

She said it more for herself than him, still waiting for her beating heart to settle down.

He scrutinised the newcomers. 'They might be part of it, the military cunningly disguised as pensioners.' He took out his phone and wiped his hand across it. 'At least this is working and didn't get damaged in the water.'

Ella leant into him. 'Check if there are any new notifications about the viaduct on the DAM website. I'll check online and see if there's any mention of what happened to us.'

They went through their phones together. Ella ignored the many notifications she'd got from the Myth-Maker app and searched on Twitter for any mentions of Saltburn.

'Nothing new has been posted,' Billy said.

'I can't find anything either,' Ella replied.

Billy wiped a bit of mud from his trousers. 'What will those soldiers do with your cousins?'

Ella sighed. 'Help them, I hope.'

She reached into her pocket and removed the card she'd taken from the fallen woman.

Billy peered at it. 'What's that?'

'That woman who was going to shoot me, it was in her hand.'

It was the size of a credit card, and they examined it together. Along the bottom was a row of dots, like a line of braille, while above that was a set of ten numbers. On the top row was one word: VENUS. The back was blank.

Billy puffed out his cheeks. 'Venus. They could be space travellers looking for aliens.'

Even though every part of Ella ached, she couldn't stop

herself from laughing. Great bursts of it pushed through her ribs, and she rocked from side to side.

'Aliens don't exist, Billy.'

He rubbed a finger over the card. 'You said that about ghosts, remember.'

Ella's laughter disappeared as quickly as it had arrived.

He's right.

She forced that thought from her mind. 'Whoever they are, how did they know we were there? And why were they only after me and the Twists and not you?'

Billy's fingers twitched and he dropped the card to the ground. 'What? How do you know that?'

'I heard the woman say it just before I knocked them out with the Light.'

'Oh,' he said. 'How did you get your Light back?'

She told him about taking it from Dotty. 'It was only a little, left over from Pandora, but it's gone now.' Ella looked down for the card, but it wasn't there. 'Crap!'

Billy jumped up, letting go of his bike so it clattered to the ground.

'There it is.'

Ella followed the direction of his pointing finger, amazed to see a ginger cat sitting opposite her with the card in its mouth.

She smiled at it. 'Nice kitty. You're pretty, aren't you?'

It gazed at her through sparkling green eyes.

Then it turned and sprinted towards the seafront.

'Damn!' Ella said as she jumped on her bike and raced after it.

She heard Billy behind her as she chased the cat thief as it ran.

If it nips into some bushes, I'll never find it.

Thankfully, it stayed on the left side, and Ella laughed

at its good road sense. There were no cars on their side, but she was approaching a junction and couldn't remember who had the right of way.

The cat didn't care and ran straight over it.

Ella heard Billy's brakes slamming hard behind her, but she stuck with the cat, pedalling over the junction as fast as she could and hoping any oncoming motorist would stop for her.

A car horn blared behind her while someone yelled, but she kept on riding with her eyes focused on the moggy.

'Wait, Ella,' Billy shouted.

But she didn't, turning off the road to follow the cat on to the pavement as it headed towards the ice cream van surrounded by kids.

More people yelled at her as she skidded around the van and gained on the thieving feline. She was getting close to it when it jumped on to a bench and turned to stare at her. Ella hit the brakes and stopped, watching the cat while realising it would only take one jump from it to get over the small wooden rail and into the grass leading down to the beach. She'd never catch it then.

And that's what it did.

Ella leapt off her bike and threw it to the ground. 'Nooooooo.'

Billy arrived as she was kicking at the back wheel.

'Where did the cat go?'

She pointed over the edge, unable to look beyond the rail.

Did the moggy do that on purpose, stealing the card from me?

Then she saw the sunlight reflecting off something on the bench.

Ella ran towards it, snatching up the card before it

vanished. It was wet and she wiped it on her trousers. She stared at it, then showed it to Billy.

'Take a photo of this in case we lose it again.'

In case I lose it again.

He did, and then she put it into her pocket.

One second later, her phone rang. She grabbed it and realised it was ten past six.

'Damn! It's my mum.'

She'd forgotten to text them about the fake flat tyre.

Billy's chest went up and down like a bouncing ball as he pointed at Ella's bike.

'Tell her you've fixed the wheel and you're on your way home.'

Which is what she did when she answered the phone.

'No, I'm okay, Mum. I didn't fall off. It was just a tricky repair.'

She listened to her mother telling her off for two minutes before she ended the call.

'What do we do next?' Billy said as Ella got on her bike.

She stared at the ocean, watching the sun sinking into the horizon.

'Stay vigilant. Don't trust anyone except me.' A flock of gulls headed out to sea, and she imagined she heard a cat meowing below her. She touched her trouser pocket and felt its contents. 'This card is the answer to who those people are, and when we find that out, we can plan our next move.'

He nodded, and then they separated. She watched him cycle into town and hoped he'd be okay without her. But, if those who'd tried to snatch them were already in Saltburn, he was in more danger than she was.

But they said they didn't want him; only me and my cousins.

And what do they know about me?

Ella left, cycling as fast as she could on her journey home to Redcar. Her fingers throbbed as she held the handlebars; her mind focused on everything around her as she went. The field was empty of cows when she rode past it this time, and she was thankful for that. The last thing she needed was groups of animals or insects swarming near her.

She exited the track into Marske, still careful of everything, with crazy ideas of soldiers popping out of nowhere to grab her. Even though she preferred to keep off the road, she stuck to it this time as it was the quicker route. And it wasn't because she was worried what her mum and dad would say about her being late; she was concerned something else might go wrong.

As she got to the roundabout, there was a noise above her head which she thought was a helicopter. She couldn't look up, with her focus on the road and the cars on either side of her, but once she was past it, she pedalled on to the pavement. She kept on cycling as she glanced above her, expecting soldiers to drop from the sky at any moment.

Paratroopers, that's what they'd be.

Relief dripped out of her when she saw it was only a light aeroplane, which she'd seen in the area before.

But it still could be them. If they're the military or the government, they could take over a local plane, and we'd know nothing about it.

They could even take over the whole town and we wouldn't know.

Everywhere she looked, Ella imagined the surrounding people were in uniforms, waiting to pounce on her. Or they were in camouflage, hiding in the bushes and the trees.

She kept on going and ignored her doubts and crazy

thoughts, but the more she dismissed them, the more new ones popped into her brain.

The card in my pocket, whatever it's for, those soldiers are bound to come looking for it. So maybe I should have left it with that cat.

The image of the moggy grinning at her was burned into the back of her skull as she reached home. She got off the bike, got her keys and opened the garage. Even then, she expected a uniformed soldier to jump out at her.

When they didn't, she put the bike away and locked the garage.

Then Ella took a deep breath and stepped into the house.

And wondered what she'd do after her parents told her off.

Ella got up late again on Sunday, not feeling hungry enough for breakfast, knowing she'd get something when she met Billy. He'd texted her at nine o'clock, wanting to meet when she was ready.

'Okay,' she'd said when she rang him. 'But not in Salt-burn. It's too dangerous there at the moment. I'll tell my parents I'm going to the car boot sale on the racecourse. My Mum hates those things so she won't want to come with me and Dad is off to the allotment. So meet me there about half one.'

She had a quick shower, and then got dressed. Her parents hadn't quizzed her much when she'd got back yesterday, but she'd felt her mother's eyes on her during their meal. Ella had expected her mum to tell her to put her clothes in the washing basket, and then go through them and find the card in her trousers.

She'd pictured her parents scowling at her, wondering what this new thing was to go with the cigarettes they'd found.

They'd think I stole it, that I'm a thief and a smoker.

But she was a thief because she took the card from that woman she'd knocked out with the burst of Light.

Throughout their evening meal, Ella had battled with the idea of telling her parents what had happened and revealing that the Twist girls were alive. But she couldn't do it.

I'd only put them in harm's way, just like I've done with Billy.

She got down on her knees and reached under the bed. There were several boxes full of games and toys, things her mum and dad had brought from London; bits of a childhood she didn't feel part of anymore.

Ella stretched her arm out as far as it would go, pushing past dolls and a Rubik's Cube she'd thought lost. Then, finally, she found the box she wanted and dragged it out. She ran her fingers over the top and stared at it.

I should push it back and forget about it. Forget about what happened yesterday.

She left it and reached under the bed again. Ella pulled out the Rubik's Cube and saw it was as messed up as her life. She solved the puzzle in ten seconds before throwing it on to the bed.

Then she returned to the box.

It was as big as her pillow and she opened it. On top were loads of photos she'd taken of London. She pushed them aside and grabbed the thing at the bottom. Then she made sure the chair was still up against the bedroom door, so nobody could walk in, before removing the Book of All Life from the box.

Ella propped her back against the bed. She stared at the door and ran her fingers over the front of the book. Then she opened it to the middle and removed the card she'd placed there last night.

Ten numbers and one word: 2900572988 and VENUS.

She hadn't had time to examine the card after they'd finished the meal, only able to hide it in the box before she'd changed her clothes. Then her mother had called her downstairs and they'd watched TV together, the three of them.

Then Ella had read for a bit, a book about twin sisters who didn't know the other existed, before going to bed at eleven. It took a while for her to get to sleep, with her mind full of memories of ghosts, the return of her cousins, and how they wanted to kill her. Plus the surprise appearance of the uniformed people with their guns.

And every time she felt like she was nodding off, that cat would come along with the card in its mouth and wink at her.

This was why she kept yawning as she ran her fingers over the card.

It's the only lead we have, but what can we do with it?

Ella shrugged as she put it in her pocket. Then she returned the Book of All Life to its hiding place, grabbed her phone, and went downstairs.

'Do you want anything to eat, love?' her dad said as he peeled some carrots.

She shook her head. 'I'll get something at the boot sale.'

Her mother grimaced as she lifted a cup of coffee to her lips.

'I thought all they had there were those burger vans you hate?'

'They have veggie options now,' Ella lied.

Gemma Finn dropped two sugars into her drink. 'Well, you make sure you have something while you're out. And take a proper bike lock with you. I've heard of people having their bikes stolen from outside the racecourse.'

Ella glanced at her father, whose cheeks had transformed into the same colour as the vegetables in his hand. Six months ago, he'd gone to the boot sale with his daughter, and they'd chained their bikes to the railings outside the entrance to the racecourse. Only he'd forgotten to lock his, and when they went back to them, his wasn't there.

'I will, Mum.'

She kissed them both on the cheek and went for her bike. The VENUS card was tucked in between two five-pound notes in her pocket. Then she checked the time on her phone and texted Billy to tell him she'd be there in fifteen minutes.

It was a relaxed ride for her. Only occasionally did she glance into the sky to ensure nothing was following her, animal, insect, or human-made. When she got there, she spotted Billy's bike in the usual spot. She chained hers next to his, happy to see a few other bikes locked to the railings.

They're much better than mine if someone is going to nick one. Especially the one with the skulls painted on the frame.

Ella took a pound coin from her pocket for the entrance fee and joined the end of the queue. It didn't take long to get inside, only a minute. She ignored the sellers at the front and searched for Billy. She couldn't see him, so she set off bargain hunting.

The first few sellers appeared to have brought nothing but scrap metal with them, so she moved beyond them. Then there was the woman who seemed to be selling all the clothes she owned and the old man with hundreds of records stuck into dusty boxes. Finally, she stopped at the next one, which had two boxes of books. Ella bent and felt her knees creak against the insides of her jeans.

It must be all the cycling.

She rifled through the books, gazing at curious covers which gave nothing away about the genre. Some of them looked like horror titles, with blood-fanged vampires and hairy werewolves on them. Others could only have been thrillers since every cover featured the back of a person staring into a vast city or the wilderness. A few of them seemed interesting. As far as she could tell, *The Killing Moon* wasn't a werewolf story, but she doubted she could get it into the house without her parents discovering it. And she knew what her mother would say.

'You're too young to read books like that, Ella.'

God knows what she'd do if she found out I'd watched all those horror movies at Billy's.

She sighed, about to stand when she spotted something curious at the back of the box: not a book, but a map. Ella grabbed it and dug it out from behind a copy of *The Exorcist.*

'*The Great British Folklore and Superstition Map.*'

The cover was shiny to the touch and smelt like tomato ketchup.

Ella stood and opened the map. It was huge, illustrated from top to bottom, with over a thousand folklore, and superstition-related locations. She fiddled with it until she found the northeast of England. The closest things she could see to where she lived were the water hag, Peg Powler from the River Tees, and a few ghosts in Middlesbrough.

I should get in touch with the publishers. I could tell them a few stories of the area for their next edition.

She returned the map to its proper shape and moved towards the sellers' table. A middle-aged woman with a shock of blue hair stood there, chewing on a giant doughnut.

'How much for the map?' Ella said.

The air smelt of sugar as the woman squinted at her and

leant forward, pushing a grumpy looking bloke out of the way. He grimaced at her and Ella guessed they were married.

'Oh, that's a good one you got there, kid. It will be worth a lot of money soon.'

Ella sighed. 'Why?'

Bits of doughnut stuck to the woman's teeth as she opened her mouth.

'Why? Haven't you been paying attention to what's happening in the world, kid? The monsters are here, and they're coming for everyone. That map in your hand contains valuable information about where the monsters are and what they do. It should be in every school, that should.'

Ella gripped a pound coin between her fingers, guessing the woman was justifying the price she was about to put on the map.

'If it's so valuable, why are you selling it?'

'Ha!' She spat bits of doughnut all over the table. 'I don't need that because I've got this.' She pulled the zip down on her jumper and showed Ella what she was wearing underneath: a Destroy All Monsters T-shirt.

Ella gritted her teeth. 'You're part of that group?'

The woman nodded. 'There're loads of us now, kid. You should join. We're everywhere.' Bits of sugar stuck to her chin. 'So I'll take a pound for the map.'

Ella slapped the coin on the table and turned from the seller with dreadful hygiene and terrible shirt. She was fuming inside as she dodged people and ignored the other sellers, reluctant to look up in case everyone around her was part of the DAM conspiracy.

Then things got worse as she approached the burger van, smelling the fumes of burnt flesh descend upon her like a claustrophobic blanket. Smoke drifted over her eyes as she stumbled towards the fence at the end of the racecourse. She flopped down when she got there, fighting back the bile bubbling in the pit of her belly.

Ella used the map to swat away the smoke, wondering if she'd taken the DAM people too lightly. She got out her phone and did an internet search, shocked at how many times she found a mention of the name online. There was a Japanese film from the 1960s with the same title, plus an American band. But most of the web pages were to do with the new lot, the ones who wanted to, in their words, "keep the world human."

No room for animals or anything else, then.

She put the phone away without looking at the search results. Then she scrutinised the people in the boot sale, sellers and buyers alike, wondering how many would see something they didn't understand and react violently to it.

The idea of it depressed her as she looked for Billy amongst the crowd. His bike was outside, so he had to be somewhere.

Then a terrible thought gripped her.

What if those soldiers grabbed him before he got inside?

Ella slapped herself hard on the leg.

I spent all that time thinking they'd be in uniforms when they came after us, but it's more likely they'll be wearing regular clothes like secret agents.

She dropped the map and placed her head in her hands. She'd been so sure Billy would be safe from those people because they were only after her.

And she was wrong. Again.

She'd put others at risk. Again.

Ella removed her hands and stared at the map on the ground. She left it there and pulled the VENUS card from her pocket.

I bet they want this back and are holding Billy hostage for it.

I'll do that. I'll give them this stupid card to get him back.

Her veins were on fire and she wanted to throw the card over the fence behind her. But she knew she couldn't. Not if she wanted to help Billy.

How do I do that? I don't know where these people are.

'You look smaller than I expected.'

Ella jerked her face up to see a shadow looming over her.

12 MY PERFECT COUSIN

Ella peered up at a tall teenage girl who'd folded her arms and was chewing gum. The sun obscured what Ella could see, so she got up. The map was at her feet as she stared at the new arrival, whose purple hair was short and spiky, with bits of green in it to match her eyes.

Green eyes. Like that cat.

The teenager blew her gum into a bubble and turned to the side. Ella saw the tattoo of a dragon on her shoulder and thought the secret agents had arrived to arrest her.

That was until the girl spoke.

'She's over here, Billy, ya daft get.'

Billy Pudding ran towards Ella, his hands full with two plastic bags of stuff.

'Ella, we've been looking everywhere for you.'

Ella turned her head from the sun. 'Who's we?'

He dropped his bags, and Ella noticed the toy cars and figurines at the top of them.

'This is my cousin, Hannah. Hannah Beard.'

Ella put a hand on her chest to stop the laughter from getting out.

'Beard?'

Hannah Beard pushed her face into Ella's. 'You got a problem with that, Finn?'

Billy stepped in between them. 'Now, now, girls, don't be fighting over me.'

They turned together to glare at him.

Hannah slapped Ella on the back. 'You thought my little cousin was called Pudding, didn't ya?'

A ripple went down Ella's spine and she did her best to ignore it.

'No, of course not. I just couldn't remember his proper surname.'

Hannah punched Ella in the shoulder, and it wasn't a light punch either.

'How long have ya been mates with the scrote?'

Ella didn't know what a scrote was, but she guessed it wasn't a compliment.

'Over a year.'

The green-eyed teenager gripped her stomach and let out a huge laugh. Then she turned to Billy.

'Did you keep the receipt when you met her, Bonzo?'

He ignored her and pointed at Ella's feet. 'What's that?'

Ella grabbed the map and told the story of how she'd bought it.

'I thought everyone here might be a DAM member.'

Hannah spat gum on to the ground. 'Them! What a bunch of cranks and crooks they are. One of the little snot rags tried to sell me a plastic gun last week.'

Billy scooped up the few miniature cars which had fallen out of his bags.

'Why are they crooks?'

His cousin tugged at her purple hair. 'Have you been on their website? When you get past the fake sightings and bigoted ramblings, you'll find the bits where they ask for membership fees and donations. If you send them fifty quid, they promise to stop mermaids trying to get into the country.'

Ella was about to reply when two lads not much older than Hannah, about eighteen, intervened.

'What you on about, girl? DAM are the only people keeping this country safe.'

They looked like brothers to Ella: one a foot taller than the other, with his cheek wobbling. The other one opened his mouth to highlight more gaps than teeth. When he spoke, Ella could smell the sea coming out of him. And not in a good way.

'Yeah, we'll protect ya girls. Better than the squirt ya'r with.'

Ella dug her nails into her palms, but Hannah spoke before she did.

'The doctors dropped you lads on your heads in the hospital, didn't they?' She poked the smaller one in the shoulder. 'Nobody could be this stupid without medical intervention or years of malpractice.'

He went to grab her, but the other lad held him back.

'Don't bother with the skank, Tommy. She and the others will come begging for our help, for the DAM soldiers, when the monsters are after them.'

'Soldiers?' Ella said.

'See?' the taller one said. 'Once the little ladies know there are men in uniform around, they get all excited.' He smirked at Ella. 'Ain't that true, love?'

She narrowed her eyes at him. 'Are you soldiers with DAM?' They didn't look old enough, but she couldn't be sure.

'Sure, girly. I'm Corporal Jack Spratt. Do ya wanna see my badge?'

They laughed together, Tommy and Jack, attracting the attention of people walking by.

Billy puffed out his cheeks and stuck his chest out at them. 'We don't need no stinkin' badges.'

Jack wiped a tear from his eye. 'What's that, squirt? Some stupid quote from a stupid movie only squirts watch?'

Ella gripped onto the map. 'Were you at the viaduct last night, about six o'clock?'

Jack finished laughing and peered at her. 'Is that where you girls hang out? We can meet you there later if ya want, bring some booze and fags. Only for you two, though, not the squirt.'

Hannah lifted her hand and poked him in the chest. 'If you were a burger at McDonald's, I'd send ya back.' Then she turned to Tommy. 'And you, you're an inspiration to idiots everywhere.'

They stood there and glared at her, looking as if they needed to get to the toilet. Jack looked like he'd throw a punch until some kid bumped into his leg. The teenager grimaced at the interloper before an adult dragged the kid away.

Tommy grabbed his brother. 'Come on. They'll keep for later.'

They skulked off and Billy breathed a sigh of relief. 'No wonder your ma hates this place, Ella.'

'Do you know them?' she said.

He shook his head. 'Never saw them before today, and I hope I don't see them again.' He looked at his cousin. 'They must have been attracted to Hannah's tattoo.'

She tried to punch him, but he dodged her fist. 'Maybe they were after all those toys you bought.'

He gripped the bags in his hands. 'Nah, this is quality stuff. It's far too good for moops like that.'

Ella stuck her hand out. 'It's nice to meet you, Hannah Beard.'

The older girl dropped another piece of chewing gum in her mouth and grinned. Then she shook Ella's hand.

'Likewise, Magic Girl.'

Ella let go of her. 'What?'

Hannah chewed and spoke at the same time. 'Don't worry, babes. My little cousin has no secrets from me, and he told me all about you and your adventures with magical creatures. Though I have to say if he'd mentioned this a year ago, I wouldn't have believed it, but with all the strange junk going on in the world, my mind is wide open.' She blew out a bubble until it burst with a large bang. 'Still, I've seen lots of weird stuff online during my hacking tours of the planet, so I'd believe anything now.'

Ella scowled at Billy. 'Why did you do that?'

He dropped his bags again and went to touch her arm, but she pulled back from him. He looked sheepish as he spoke.

'I'm sorry, Ella. I know I should've asked you first, but Hannah can help us.'

Ella looked at his cousin. 'How?'

Hannah swallowed her gum and pointed a finger at Ella as if her hand were a gun.

'Because I've cracked the mystery of that card you found last night.' She glanced over at Jack and Tommy, who continued to scowl at them from the other side of the boot sale. 'And I'm guessing it's got nothing to do with those bozos.'

Ella lowered her voice to a near whisper. 'How... how did you do that?'

Hannah removed a mobile phone from her pocket and showed Ella the screen.

'Cousin Billy showed me the photo he took of that card, and I used my considerable computer skills to discover what it is.'

Ella put a hand on her heart to steady her breathing. 'We can't talk about it here.'

Hannah grinned, exposing the purple stain on her teeth from the gum.

'Great, cos I'm starving. There's a fantastic chippy near the seafront. So we'll go there and you can buy us some scran.'

Ella crossed her arms. 'Why am I buying?'

Hannah laughed. 'Well, that's cos Bonzo Billy spent all his money on toys, and you owe me for the risks I took cracking the mystery of the card you stole off the dead soldier.'

Ella gasped. 'She wasn't dead.'

The purple-haired teenager leant into Ella. 'How do you know, kid? Bonzo told me you ran away after you fired your fancy magic at them. They could all be dead as far as you know, including your manky cousins.'

'It's not magic.' The blood was boiling inside Ella and she needed ice cream to cool down. 'It's energy and it's all scientific.'

Hannah rolled her eyes. 'If you say so, but Cousin Billy tried to describe it to me, and I thought his head was going to explode.' She winked at him. 'And how would I explain that to me aunt and uncle?'

Ella pushed past them. 'I need a lemon top.' Then she stormed off and expected them to follow her.

They did, with Hannah blowing kisses to the red-faced Tommy and Jack as the girls and Billy left the car boot sale.

Ella went to her bike, seeing that Hannah had one chained next to Billy's: the one with the skulls painted on it.

It was a ten-minute ride from the racecourse to the seafront. Ella never said a word, letting Billy do all the talking. He must have apologised to her at least two dozen times by the time they reached the ice cream parlour.

'Don't you want some fish and chips first?' Hannah said.

Ella hadn't fifteen minutes earlier, but when she got there, that had changed. Smelling the fried food awakened the hunger that had slumbered in her belly since she'd left home with no breakfast.

She put the map into her pocket. 'Okay. We'll get some and eat it on the beach. How does that sound?'

Hannah slapped her on the back again, and Ella wondered how long it would be before she smacked the girl in the face.

'That's great.' Then she grinned at Billy. 'What do you think, Pudding?'

He nodded. 'If that's okay with you, Ella. I'll pay you back next week.'

Ella stared at him. 'I know you will, Bonzo.'

FIFTEEN MINUTES LATER, they were sitting on the beach, stuffing their faces with hot fish and chips, but without the fish for Ella. Hannah had drenched hers with salt and vinegar, and the smell of it appeared to be attracting all the birds nearby.

Hannah eyed them suspiciously. 'Is this your doing, Magic Girl?' She munched on a massive piece of fish as she spoke. 'Billy said the insects and animals have been behaving oddly around you.'

Ella threw a few chips into the sand and the gulls flew towards them.

'I told you, Purple Girl, it's not magic.'

The birds fought over the food as Hannah spoke.

'Okay, it's all to do with Elementals and the Light, and you're the special girl who controls it all.'

Ella sighed. 'That will do for now. So tell me what you found out about the Venus card.'

Hannah finished her grub and looked ready to throw the plastic container into the sand until Ella scowled at her. Instead, she dropped it into Billy's lap.

'Well, I had to delve into the dark web first. Do you know what that is?'

'Sure,' Billy said. 'It's what me ma is always warning me about.'

Ella laughed. 'And your ma is right because it's where criminals and dodgy people go to do their dodgy deals.'

'It's more than that,' Hannah said. 'Through the dark web, private computer networks can communicate and conduct business anonymously without divulging identifying details, such as a user's location. And that means it's a place where hackers like me can connect with other hackers to get the information I can't.'

Ella removed the VENUS card from her pocket. 'So you used the dark web to discover what this is?'

Billy stuck a greasy chip into his mouth. 'She hasn't told me yet, but I bet it's to do with ancient aliens.'

'Ancient aliens?' Ella said.

Billy's eyes sparkled as he spoke. 'You know that ETs came to Earth thousands of years ago and built the pyramids and stuff.'

Hannah reached out her hand and pushed her cousin into the sand.

'Don't be daft, ya silly bugger. Aliens don't exist, and even if they did, why would they waste their time with our spawny species?'

Billy brushed himself down, but didn't answer her.

'What did you discover?' Ella said.

'Well,' Hannah said, 'I used the photo the daft bugger took of the VENUS card and shared it with some of my colleagues on the dark web. The ten dots and the numbers on the card appear to be security codes to enter a system or a building. And it looks like VENUS is the name of the person the card belongs to.'

Ella kicked her feet into the sand. 'I'd already guessed all that.'

Hannah waved a finger at her. 'Is that so, little grasshopper? Did you also guess where the building which the card gets you into is?'

Ella's lips trembled. 'No.'

'Well, I found out.' Hannah stood and pointed. 'It's somewhere over there.'

'That's the old steelworks,' Billy said.

Ella got up and looked at where she was pointing.

'And that's where I'm going.'

13   FEED THE TREE

'We can't go there,' Billy said.

The three of them were standing on the promenade with their bikes. Ella looked at him.

'Why? Because you want to get ice cream?'

Billy grimaced at her. 'No. The steelworks have been closed for ages, but there are people over there cleaning the place up.'

Ella knew what he meant. 'I know. I saw it in the news, but we can still check it out.' She stared at Hannah. 'What do you think?'

Hannah shrugged. 'It's either that or go home to watch Bonzo play with his toy cars.'

Ella laughed, while Billy scowled at his cousin. They got on their bikes and cycled out of Redcar, riding on the pavement and annoying the pedestrians. Ella led the way through Coatham, past the marshes and on to the path running parallel to the Trunk Road. She glanced over the bridge to see a group of swans drifting on the water.

Every time she lifted her legs to pedal, she felt the VENUS card in her pocket. Billy and Hannah were behind her, riding side by side. She could hear them talking, but not what they said.

Why did Billy tell her about what I've done with the Book of All Life and Elementals?

It had annoyed her at first, until she realised having someone else to share her secrets with could be a good thing. And Hannah was older than them, so she'd probably had different experiences that might be helpful. Ella had learnt much during her time in the multiverse and had grown up a lot, but at sixteen, Billy's cousin acted like an adult, especially when dealing with those two lads at the boot sale. And having another girl around would be a good thing, so her anger at Billy had passed. Not that she'd let him know it yet.

Ella was wondering what she'd talk about with Hannah apart from Light and Elementals when the entrance to the steelworks appeared ahead. She stopped before the others and stared at the place hiding the secrets of their attackers from yesterday.

'Crikey,' Billy said. 'We'll never get in there.'

Ella examined the front gate with its barriers and uniformed security.

'I thought they'd have cleared the site by now.'

Hannah laughed like a hyperactive chipmunk. 'There are six hundred acres here and decades' worth of construction to remove, and then they have to make the land safe for new industries. You've got a blast furnace and coke works to dismantle, as well as the chimneys and other buildings. Then you have to make sure the soil isn't polluted and clean everything to meet environmental standards.'

Billy and Ella looked at her as if she'd swallowed an encyclopaedia.

'How do you know all this?' Ella said.

'My grandfather worked here for thirty years before moving to Leeds.' She tapped the side of her head. 'When I was little, he told me loads of stories of what it was like working in the main plant, about the unbearable heat and the danger. And of all the weird things he saw.'

'Grandad Sammy?' Billy said.

Hannah nodded. 'Aye. He used to call me HBB and let me take a drag of his cigs.'

'HBB?' Ella said.

Billy laughed. 'Did he name you after a pencil?'

She scowled at her cousin. 'Hannah Big Brain because I was the cleverest in the family. And I was always top of my classes in school. So I might be the first Beard to go to university.'

'That's impressive,' Ella said. 'But what do you mean about the weird things he saw in the steelworks?'

Hannah lowered her head to the handlebars. 'Well, he wasn't sure if parts of the plant where he worked were haunted, but he saw stuff he couldn't explain.'

Billy's eyes were ready to explode. 'Such as?'

They pulled their bikes closer to Hannah as she spoke.

'He said there was something strange about the place, but it was hard to tell because of the conditions, with the heat, and what the workers had to wear. So, he'd been there a few years, and I think he was about twenty when he had his first weird encounter.

'Grandad Sammy was nearing the end of a long shift, after about ten hours or summat, when he saw a glow on the floor, all orange and shiny. He was wary as he moved towards it, thinking it might have been molten steel, but there was no heat coming off it. And, as he got closer, he heard the noise.'

A truck roared past them on the road and Billy nearly fell off his bike.

'What kind of noise?'

Hannah stared at her cousin. 'Grandad said it was like a radio where you can't find the right station.' She shook her head. 'I didn't know what he meant and told him, so he said to imagine walking down a street, and you hear someone singing to you, maybe even calling your name. It gets louder as you get closer, but you can't see who's singing. And then it would suddenly stop.'

Ella relaxed her grip on the bike. 'That sounds like, after a long shift, he heard things that weren't there, hallucinating because he was so tired.'

Hannah nodded. 'That's what I said, but he had more tales.' She looked around the path that was empty apart from them. 'About six months after that, he heard voices under the ground in the same spot. He put his head to the floor, and at least two people were talking in a strange language.'

'Did he tell anyone at work?' Ella said.

'He told a couple of people, but they only laughed at him and said he was a nutter. So after that, he kept all his other encounters to himself.'

Billy whistled loudly. 'How many were there?'

Hannah narrowed her eyes. 'Well, he worked there for thirty years, so there must have been loads, but I don't think he told me all of them.'

'Why not?'

'He probably didn't want to scare me. But I remember the scariest one.'

'Go on,' Ella said.

Hannah sat up straight on her bike. 'It was in the last few years of his time at the steelworks. He thought he heard voices again, but they were coming from a wall this time. He couldn't hear what they were saying, so he walked towards it, but something made him stop when he was only a few feet away. He didn't know what it was, but it probably saved his life that night.'

'Blimey,' Billy said. 'Was it to do with the hot steel?'

'No,' Hannah said. 'Grandad told me he was close to the wall when it moved, or something shifted inside of it like ripples on top of a river. Then, as he stared at it, a hand shot out and tried to get him. Only it wasn't human, but green and slimy with long nails ready to claw his face. He stood there transfixed - that was his word - unable to move. He watched it trying to grab him, and then all the fingers shimmered, and when they came back into focus, there was a blaring red eyeball on the end of each one.'

She paused for breath, and all three of them were deathly silent.

Then she continued. 'The eyes blinked at him as a mouth appeared in the middle of the palm and spoke to Grandad.'

Ella gulped. 'What did it say?'

'Only one word,' Hannah said. '"Sammy."'

Ella put a hand to her face, remembering what had happened to her in the Twist house.

Bad memories haunt you forever.

Billy looked over at the entrance to the steelworks. 'It might be a good thing we can't get in there.'

Ella shook her head. 'I need to find out why the VENUS card leads to here. We could try getting in from the other side, from the road leading to the gare.'

'That's no good,' Hannah said. 'It has a tall metal fence around it over there.'

Billy seemed pleased by that. 'Then we're scuppered.'

Hannah placed a hand on his shoulder. 'You don't get out of it that easily, little cousin. I know another way in, one our grandfather told me about.' She pulled her bike away from them. 'Follow me.'

She rode back the way they'd come before stopping by the side of a low wooden fence separating the path and the trees. Hannah got off her bike and strode towards the fence. Ella and Billy followed her.

'We can't get in that way,' Billy said. 'There's a wide beck running through the trees.'

Hannah put her arm around his shoulder and squeezed. 'Well, you can stay here and mind the bikes, little cousin.' Then she glanced at Ella. 'Because me and Magic Girl are going in now.'

Billy huffed and puffed and rubbed at his chin. 'Okay. I'll come with you. But what about the bikes? Shall we lock them to this fence?'

Hannah shook her head. 'No. If we do that, they'll be visible from the road. We don't want anyone seeing them and wondering what's going on. So once we climb over, we'll hide them in the bushes.'

'What about the beck?' Ella said. She had visions of what had happened at the viaduct, her cousins striding through the water to kill her.

Hannah grinned. 'You've fought monsters and soldiers, and a little bit of water scares you?'

Before Ella could reply, the older girl lifted her bike over the fence. Ella looked at Billy, seeing the nervousness in his eyes. She was about to tell him to stay there when he followed his cousin into the trees.

Ella picked up her bike. She sucked air into her lungs as she got over, dropping her bike with the others behind a tree. Billy had left his bags of new toys there as well.

The beck smelt filthy and she flapped at the flies swarming around her head. Then the three of them stepped into it. The water came up to Ella's knees and turned her legs cold.

Billy sighed. 'Me ma's gonna kill me when I get home with dirty kecks.'

Ella trudged through the liquid to reach the other side, digging her fingers into the mud to climb up to the trees on that side. Then she wiped her hands on her trousers and stared through the branches at the large grey building in front of them.

She stood next to Hannah. 'You said there are six hundred acres on the site. So how are we going to find the entrance for the VENUS card?'

The older girl smiled at her. 'I'm hoping this Light you keep talking about will show you the way.'

'Brilliant.' Ella was pushing her way through the trees when Billy grabbed her arm.

'Look at the ground, Ella.'

She did and saw it moving. The mud, leaves, and branches rose and fell to match the rhythm of her heart. The three of them moved back, only to find the same behind them.

Hannah gripped Ella's other arm. 'The ground's alive.'

Billy gasped. 'It's like Grandad said: things are living underneath here.'

They stood there frozen as Ella waited for the slimy hand to shoot out of the ground and pull them under the earth.

E lla was frozen for only a second. Then she kicked at the moving leaves to reveal what was underneath them.

'Rats!' Billy shouted.

Hannah stopped him before he ran. 'Don't move, cousin.' She peered at the skittering mass. 'I don't think they're interested in us, but let's not take the risk.'

The rat army headed for Ella, circling her in a continuous motion. They nibbled at the leaves as they moved, dripping saliva onto the ground. A pungent smell of rotten food drifted from them and up to her. She put a hand over her nose and grimaced.

Ratter, is this because I let you down?

She watched as the rats stopped moving and peered at her through shimmering eyes.

'We could run back to the water,' Billy said. 'They won't follow us in there.'

'There's no need,' Ella said. 'They're focused on me. So you two can keep going while I lead them away.'

Hannah grabbed her hand. 'Nah, we stick together, kid.

Look at their faces; they're not here to attack you: this is worship. You're the rat queen.'

Ella gritted her teeth. 'Great.'

She stepped forward and the rats separated to let her through. Billy and Hannah strode by her side until they came out of the trees. Ella turned to see the rat army gazing at her.

Then Billy fell to the ground, clutching his chest. 'You'll give me a heart attack one day, Ella.'

She took his hand and pulled him up. 'Not today, my friend.' She peered at the grey building opposite them. 'Let's look in there first.'

They ran across the pavement to the front. There was noise coming from the other direction, and Ella guessed it came from those tasked with clearing the site. They jumped into the shadows and looked at the entrance. She was prepared to use her house-breaking experience to get into the building, but she didn't have to: the door was unlocked.

She pushed it open and led Billy and Hannah inside to a long, empty corridor. Dust floated in the air, and it smelt of unemptied bin bags. The three of them stayed together as they checked the rooms: old calendars hung from the walls, still set on the days when the last people had worked in the building. Grime and mould were everywhere, sprouting out from the ground and crawling over wood and concrete. The largest room contained tables covered with discarded coffee cups and bits of cutlery. Buckets of dirty water stood around the edge of the skirting boards, attracting flies by the dozen. Other insects scuttled over the floor and the walls.

Ella swiped a fly away from her head. 'Welcome to the ghost town.'

She went to a stack of cabinets, opening the drawers to find abandoned papers and broken pens. She found discarded keyboards, computer equipment, and even a table with a single shoe on it in the next room. Someone had also left birthday cards dumped in a chair.

Hannah picked up the shoe. 'Is Cinderella one of your Elementals?'

Bits of paper, wires, folders and files lay scattered over the floor, joined by empty plastic bottles and broken mugs. They checked every room and found nothing useful.

Billy sneezed near the stairs. 'Should we go up?'

Ella removed the VENUS card from her pocket. 'No. I don't think the card has anything to do with this place. We have to check outside.'

'Is your Elemental radar working?' Hannah said.

Ella shook her head. 'We need to go where the people are.' She looked at them. 'You wouldn't have a security card for an empty building.'

They returned to the entrance and stepped outside.

'Where to?' Billy said.

Ella pointed at a car heading for the far side of the site. 'That way.'

She started walking and the others followed, with Billy leaning into her.

'What happens if we get caught?'

She smiled at him. 'Don't worry. We'll say we were exploring, as kids do. I mean, what's the worst they can do to us? They won't arrest three teenagers, will they?'

Hannah popped a piece of gum in her mouth without offering them any. 'The coppers locked me up once for sleeping in a disused railway building. They kept me in a cell all night, trying to scare some sense into me, they said.'

Billy stared at his cousin. 'Why were you there?'

She grinned at him. 'It was for a bet. The place was supposed to be haunted. I got twenty quid for kipping there.' Hannah rolled her tongue over the top of her lip. 'But I think one kid dobbed me in to the fuzz.'

'That won't happen here,' Ella said.

Hannah chewed on her gum. 'If those soldiers are here, they'll snatch us and lock us up.'

'They'll have to tell our parents, though, won't they?' Billy said. 'You can't just lock people up without evidence and stuff.'

'Don't be naïve, little cousin. There are all kinds of black ops that go on. And kids go missing all the time. Three more in a cold northern town won't make much difference. With everything that's going on at the moment, I bet we wouldn't even make the news.'

They stuck to the shadows and followed the route the car had taken. It was gone from their view, and no more had appeared. Bits of steel of all sizes lay everywhere, joined by rubble, weeds, grass, and the occasional plastic bottle. Ella thought she could smell smoke and burning rubber.

They'd been walking for ten minutes when she heard voices coming from the building closest to them. She pulled Billy and Hannah down so they were crouching close to the ground. Ella put a finger to her lips as three people in uniforms came out and turned the corner.

'They look like the same uniforms that attacked us at the viaduct,' Billy whispered.

Ella nodded. 'They are.' She grabbed her friends' hands. 'I'm going to sneak inside, but there's still time for you two to leave.'

Hannah blew her gum into a bubble before sucking it into her mouth. 'You're right, kid. Someone needs to go back to let the police know what happened to you.' She turned to Billy. 'So I nominate Bonzo.'

The fire burned inside Billy's eyes and Ella thought he'd explode.

'You wouldn't be here without me, cousin, and I'm not going anywhere.'

Hannah placed a hand on his shoulder. 'Wonderful.' Then she stared at Ella. 'But we need a plan before we go inside.'

'You're right,' Ella said. 'And I've got one.' She gazed at the columns of metal around them, peering at the pipes and beams that snaked everywhere like thick metallic spaghetti. Then she looked at him. 'Billy, you're the smallest and quickest of us. Do you think you can sneak into the building?' He nodded. 'Great. Get into the front and use your phone to send me a video of what it's like in there. Then stay in the shadows until we decide our next move. And everyone, make sure your mobile is on silent.'

They did that. Then Billy stuck close to the ground and followed the darkness to the entrance. It took him fewer than thirty seconds to get there, but it felt like an age to Ella. In the middle of those industrial ruins, silence filled the void apart from the sound of Ella's heart beating like a nuclear explosion in her head.

A minute later, she received a video call from him. Hannah crouched behind her as Ella answered. It was dark inside, but she saw massive metal constructs, things that looked like giant rusted buckets, and great steel containers. There were pools of water on the floor and piles of rubble everywhere, but no sign of any living thing.

'There's nobody here,' Billy whispered into the phone.

It was all Ella needed to hear. She slipped the mobile into her pocket, and Hannah and she scuttled across the opening and into the building. Billy was crouching in the corner when they got there.

Ella lowered her voice. 'Okay. We all stay together and stick to the shadows until we know what's going on.'

Light filtered in through gaps in the roof and windows. Ella twisted her head to look up, staggered by the size of the place. It must have been two hundred feet tall, and as she walked through it, she imagined she was in the land of the giants as one of the tiny people.

The ground was dark, dirty, and dusty as she stepped across it. She peered at the metal stands around her, trying to imagine what it would have been like when they were working, blasting out heat and molten steel.

'It's like being in a science-fiction movie,' Billy said in hushed tones.

Hannah grinned. 'Are you still looking for your aliens, little cousin?'

Ella smiled as well. The place was impressive and daunting, but she felt no connection to Light or Elementals in the building. And there was no sign of any soldiers.

Maybe those people we saw were part of the steelworks clean-up crew after all, security to keep intruders like us out.

She stopped walking and looked at the VENUS card again. Then she spoke to Hannah.

'Are you sure this is the right place?'

Hannah gulped down her chewing gum. 'As sure as my name is Hannah Aurelia Beard.'

Ella didn't laugh at the unusual middle name. 'How do you know?'

Hannah took the VENUS card from Ella. 'There's a chip in here, like the GPS tracking system on your phone, and it's pointing to this site. But, as I said earlier, there are six hundred acres here, so you can't expect to find the door for this key easily.'

Before Ella could reply, Billy leant into her.

'There's a light at the back of the room.'

'It's getting dark, so it's probably the sun setting or a bit of moonlight,' Hannah said.

'No,' he said. 'It's coming from the ground.'

Ella jerked her head up to see what he was talking about. She didn't notice the light at first until Billy pulled her towards him. Then she saw it, flickering illumination seeping out from underneath a giant steel bucket at the far end of the building.

She moved forward, saying nothing, feeling the blood surging through her veins and the hairs standing on the back of her neck.

There's Light down there, I'm sure of it.

They stepped through rubble and discarded bits of metal, and Ella felt the silence fall over her like a blanket. The light stayed a constant flicker as they inched closer and she saw the hole in the ground.

Billy got there first. 'There's a ladder here.'

Hannah pushed him to the side. 'The only way is down.'

Then she climbed into the hole. Ella followed, then Billy. It took a minute to get to the bottom. It was as big as where they'd just come from, but there were no extensive metal structures there, only a tent the size of a football field.

That's where the light was coming from.

'What now?' Billy said.

Ella touched his arm. 'You two stay here while I look.'

'Wait,' Hannah said. 'Someone's leaving.'

She was right, but it wasn't someone; it was a group of people.

And something.

Four uniformed blokes were holding on to a being bigger than them. It was at least eight feet tall, covered in brown hair, with dull yellow eyes. The men dragged it forward and it stumbled. A low groan escaped from it as the creature fell.

Two of the soldiers withdrew items from their belts and flicked them out, so they extended into long sticks. Then they poked the creature with the rods and sparkling blue electricity shot through it. It moaned on the ground, but didn't move. Then the four of them dragged it out of the building at the far end.

Hannah's hand trembled as she spoke. 'What was that?'

Ella dug her nails into her palm. 'That was a Bigfoot, also known as a Sasquatch.' An ache spread through every inch of her as she stared at the tent. 'There's a gap in dimensions here, and Elementals are crossing into our world through it.'

Now, what do I do about it?

15 BRITISH STEEL

Ella bent her neck, struggling to breathe. She stood like that for a minute before raising her head.

'We must help the Elementals in that tent.'

She went to move forward, but Hannah pulled her back.

'I agree, Ella, but we can't just rush in. We're three kids against armed soldiers, and God knows what else. We have to go away and think about this, come up with a plan.'

She was right, but Ella was like a cat on a hot tin roof. The muscles were bouncing in her legs and it was a struggle to keep still.

Ella bit into her top lip and peered at her hands.

'I need to get my Light back. Not just the little I got from Dotty, but near to what I had from Pandora.'

'How would you do that?' Billy said.

Ella tasted blood at the back of her throat. 'I don't know. Pandora is stuck in the multiverse, and I wouldn't want her here, anyway.' She stared at Billy. 'I could use the Book of All Life to bring Elementals to this world; ask them for their Light.'

'And create an Elemental army with them,' Hannah said.

Ella closed her eyes and questioned what she was about to do. Then she looked at her friends.

'I can't start a war here. Not without knowing what's happening in that tent.'

'No one here is at war with you, Ella Finn.'

The three of them jumped at the sound of the voice, turning to see someone walking towards them: a woman with the name VENUS stitched into her uniform.

As Ella hesitated, Billy spoke.

'Sorry, lady, we came in here to play and got lost. Can you show us the way out?'

The woman with the dark bob and ocean blue eyes offered them her hand.

'I'm Veronica Venus and I'm in charge of this operation.' She glanced at each of them. 'And you are Ella Finn, plus Billy and Hannah Beard.'

Hannah shook her hand. 'Pleased to meet you, lady. If you're the boss here, maybe you can tell me where the toilets are because I'm busting for a pee.'

'How do you know who we are?' Ella said.

Venus let go of Hannah's hand. 'Well, if you return my card, I'll give you a tour of the facility.' She grinned at Hannah and Billy. 'This will include refreshments and a bathroom.' Ella said nothing. 'Or I can have security escort you out of here and you'll never see me again.'

Ella dragged her friends from Veronica Venus. They huddled together as she whispered to them.

'What do you think? Should we go with her or get out of here?'

'I'll follow you, Ella,' Billy said.

Hannah crossed her legs and fidgeted. 'I really need to

take a pee. So if we don't go with her, I'll have to nip into the shadows for a quick leak.'

Ella shot her a nervous grin. 'That's settled then.' They separated, and she went to Venus. 'We're ready for the tour.'

Hannah jumped in front of her. 'But show me where the bogs are first.'

Venus grinned. 'There's a Portaloo behind the tent. Just go to the top and you can't miss it.'

Hannah didn't need any extra encouragement. Ella watched her run and hoped they weren't all heading into a trap. Then they set off, with Venus in the middle of Billy and her.

'Aren't you glad you didn't visit this place when it was a working blast furnace? The heat would have been unbearable right about now.'

Ella guessed this was Venus's attempt at small talk, but she wasn't interested in that.

But Billy was. 'Mine and Hannah's grandad used to work here, and he said it was like being inside a microwave in a sauna.'

Venus laughed. 'He was right. Above where we are, temperatures could get as high as two thousand degrees Celsius. The hot air blast to the furnace would burn the coke and maintain the temperature. The reaction between the air and the fuel would generate carbon monoxide, which would reduce the oxide in the ore to iron.

'Then the impurities were removed to react with calcium oxide to make a liquid slag that floated on top of the molten iron. The slag was collected after the denser iron had been run out of a tap hole near the bottom of the furnace.'

'What's all this talk about slags?' Hannah rubbed her hands as she rejoined them.

'We're getting a history of the furnace above our heads.' Ella peered at their guide. 'Did you work here, Ms Venus?'

'Please, call me Veronica. And no, unlike Samuel Beard, I never worked in here until we discovered the portal to another world.'

She stepped into the tent, and the three teenagers followed her with their mouths open wide enough to catch a fish.

'What do you mean, a portal to another world?'

Venus replied to her, but Ella didn't hear what she said since she was too busy staring at the large yellow circle in the middle of the tent. It was floating four feet off the ground and vibrating. There were dozens of men and women gathered around it, some in combat uniforms, while others wore white lab coats as if they were doctors or scientists. There was also lots of electrical equipment everywhere, including cameras and two generators.

Veronica Venus pointed at the circle. 'That's what I mean. Perhaps it's a portal not to another world, but a different dimension to ours, or even a link to the past or the future.' She turned to look at Ella. 'What do you think, Ms Finn?'

Ella put a hand over her heart. 'Me? Why would I know anything about that?'

Venus peered at her. 'Why don't we get those refreshments I mentioned, and then we can have a long chat about all of this. How does that sound?'

One part of Ella's brain told her to leave, to run away as quickly as possible. But another part knew she couldn't; she was too curious to discover what this all was.

'Okay, but I must text my parents first to let them know where I am.'

Venus smiled at her. 'Oh, there's no need for that, Ella.

I've already sent someone to reassure your mother and father you're fine.' She looked at Hannah and Billy. 'And I've done the same for you two. So now let's have something to eat. There are burgers and fries in the canteen today.' She winked at Ella. 'Including veggie burgers.'

She strode out, pursued by the Beards. Ella had a last glance at the illuminated circle before joining them.

An exit behind the tent led into a vast corridor with several rooms on either side. Venus took them to the second one on the left. Ella tried looking into the first room they walked past, but the door was closed and the blinds were down.

They stepped inside the room and it was unoccupied. Billy ran to a counter split into different sections with food behind each. He grabbed a plateful of fries and a burger and sat at the nearest table. Hannah got a Coke and a sandwich and joined him. Ella took nothing, but sat with them. She watched her friends stuffing their faces, amazed they could think of their bellies after what they'd just seen.

Venus pulled up a chair next to them. 'Aren't you hungry, Ella?'

A strained smile crept over Ella's face. 'Only for information. Who are you, who do you work for, and what is this place? And how do you know who we are?'

Veronica Venus sipped at the water she'd taken from the counter.

'My, my, that is a lot of questions.' She finished drinking and put the bottle on the table. 'As I said before, my name is Veronica Venus. I work for an organisation called the Institute. What we do is try to control the ebb and flow of the portals between our world and others, one of which you've just seen. And because of this, we've had our eye on you,

Ella Finn, and your friends because of what happened last year.'

Hannah chewed on a fat chip as she spoke. 'What happened last year?'

Venus removed a phone from her pocket. 'This did.' She turned the screen to them and played a video Ella had seen many times before: it was her, Billy, and Dora travelling with a unicorn. Then, outside the local hospital, patients gathered around the animal to touch it.

Ella shrugged. 'That video's a fake. Unicorns aren't real.'

Venus placed the phone next to the water bottle.

'Of course they are, Ella, as well you know. Sixteen people touched the unicorn that day, all of whom were ill, some with more serious ailments than others. Do you know what happened to them?'

'No,' Ella said.

'They all got better,' Venus said. 'Even the two who had terminal cancer made miraculous recoveries. The doctors had no explanation for it. If it hadn't been for another extraordinary event, I'm sure the unicorn at the hospital would have got wider media coverage.'

Ella asked even though she already knew what the answer would be.

'What extraordinary event?'

Venus moved closer to her. 'Why, Ella, that was the day you brought the monsters into our world. I'm guessing you knew these creatures had healing properties, and you were trying to do good, but it backfired, and many people got hurt. Some were killed, did you know that?'

'None of that has anything to do with Billy or me. That unicorn, real or fake, followed us from the carnival at Redcar Racecourse to the hospital.'

The chair creaked as Venus crossed her legs. 'Ah yes, the hospital. And why were you there?'

'I went to visit my cousin, Dotty. She was in a coma after an accident at school.'

Venus reached for her phone. 'An accident, you say. Do you mean this?'

She pressed on the screen and a new video played. This one was Ella fighting her cousins in the playground. And then the Elemental she'd summoned using the Book of All Life, the knocker, arrived and injured Dotty.

'How do you have this clip?' Ella said.

Venus hit pause on the app. 'You don't deny this is real?'

'No, it happened, but there weren't any cameras there.'

Venus smirked at her. 'Don't be naïve, Ella. There are cameras everywhere.' She flicked her fingers on the phone and showed Ella a photograph. 'Do you know this girl?'

A stab of electricity ran through Ella's chest. 'That's Dora.'

'Who has since disappeared,' Venus said. 'What about this person?'

The following image was of the witch Seraphina.

'I don't know her,' Ella lied.

'Okay. What about this boy?'

She showed Ella a photo of the Irish teenager who'd saved them in the barn.

'No,' she lied again.

Venus sat back in her chair and sighed.

'All right. Perhaps after I've given you a tour of what we do here, you might change your mind and start telling the truth.'

She got up and walked out. Ella didn't move.

Billy finished his food and whispered to her. 'She knows everything, Ella.'

Ella didn't reply, looking around the room and expecting hidden microphones and cameras.

But she knew Veronica Venus didn't know everything.

She doesn't know what Elementals are.

She doesn't know about the Book of All Life.

She doesn't know what Light is.

Ella got up. 'Let's see the rest of this tour.'

Whatever this place is, I have to get my Light back.

16 SHAKE THE DISEASE

Ella led them into the corridor. Venus stood in the doorway opposite, inviting them into the room. Ella entered first, noticing a large viewing area on the far wall. She went and joined Venus there, her eyes bulging wide at what she saw through the glass.

'My cousins are here?'

Daisy was sitting on a bed, writing in a notebook. Standing away from her were Dolly and Dotty, talking to two people who might have been doctors or scientists in their white uniforms.

'We thought it best to bring them here after the recovery at the viaduct,' Venus said. 'All of them are doing well, physically.'

Hannah joined them at the glass. 'They don't look like you, Ella.'

Billy stood next to her. 'There's nothing wrong with them?'

Venus turned to him. 'All of them have undergone several physical checks, including blood and DNA tests, and they appear to be three normal, typical teenagers. Apart from one thing.'

Ella took a deep breath. 'What's that?'

Venus touched a button on the wall and spoke. 'Hello, girls. I hope you are well today.' Everyone in the other room, including the adults, stopped what they were doing. 'Daisy, can you come to the window and show me what you're doing?' Venus looked at Ella. 'Don't worry. They can't see us on this side.'

Ella was wondering why that would matter when Daisy got off the bed and approached the glass. Then she held up the book so everyone could see what she'd written. The same two words filled the page.

Kill Smella.

Hannah tapped Ella on the shoulder. 'Does she mean you?'

Before Ella could reply, Dolly and Dotty left the medics and joined their sister at the window. Even on the other side of the divide, Ella felt the hate seeping from them. They thrust their hands against the glass, and Ella and Billy flinched backwards. Hannah and Venus didn't move.

'Kill Smella,' they said together.

Daisy dropped her book, and all three of them spat out the same mantra.

'Kill Smella. Kill Smella. Kill Smella.'

On and on they went, with their eyes burning into the window. Ella put both hands over her ears, but she could still hear them. When Ella took her hands from her head, Venus spoke.

'It's time for their injections, Dr Costello.'

One of the white-uniformed adults in the room, a woman, removed three needles from her pocket and used them to inject the Twist girls with a colourless liquid. Then she led them to their beds, and they lay down. Their mouths continued to move, but no sound came out of them. Instead, the skin on their faces moved and rippled as if a living thing was underneath their flesh.

Ella shivered as she placed one hand on the glass, feeling something in the other room but unsure what it was. 'What's going to happen to them?'

Venus pressed the button on the wall again. 'Physically, there's nothing wrong with them, but they have deep-rooted psychological problems. Still, we've only had them here for twenty-four hours. Once we transfer them to another facility, they'll get the best help we have, which is considerable. Some of the world's finest therapists work for the Institute, so your cousins will want for nothing. At some point, we might even reunite them with their parents.'

Ella gulped and snatched her hand from the glass. 'You know where they are?'

Venus turned from the window. 'Your Uncle George worked for a large petrochemical company as an accountant. That allowed him to embezzle a considerable amount of money from his employers. So the day the creatures - monsters, some would say - invaded the planet was the perfect opportunity for him to flee once his bosses discovered his transgressions. He and his wife, Ida, are living in South America, lounging on a beach and drinking tequila. We know where they are at all times, but the Twists are low on our priorities.'

Hannah shook her head. 'They abandoned their kids?'

Venus stared at her. 'The bond between parent and child is non-existent with some adults. From the reports I've seen, I'm not sure if they even know their daughters exist anymore. Or care.'

Ella peered at her cousins sleeping on the other side of

the glass. They looked peaceful, but she could still hear their words lurking in the shadows of her head.

'Do you think you can help them?'

Pandora did this to them, but how much blame lies with me?

Venus moved towards the door. 'Why don't I answer that by showing you what else we're doing here?'

She stepped outside, but Ella didn't follow, turning to her friends instead.

'Are you okay, Billy?'

He nodded. 'I am. At least we know what happened to your aunt and uncle now, and it looks like your cousins are being looked after.'

Yes. But why haven't these people told the police what they know about the Twists?

'Are you coming?' Venus said from the corridor.

Hannah grinned and led the way out. 'This isn't one of those psycho hospitals you see in horror films, is it? You're not going to drug us, and then do all kinds of crazy experiments on us, are you?'

Venus laughed. 'It's quite the opposite, Ms Beard.' She went to the next room and opened the door. 'I'd like you to meet Dr Petra Withe and Dr Gary Shaw, who run the medical side of this facility.'

Ella and her friends stepped into the room. It was larger than the previous one, as big as a hospital ward, and separated into sections using curtains as dividers. A bald man with a boxer's nose and a tall woman with a beautiful afro and startling eyes greeted them.

'Please, call me Petra,' the woman said as she stuck out her hand. Ella took it, impressed with the smoothness of the woman's skin and how she had the face of someone from a glossy magazine. And inside her pupils, there seemed to be a thousand shooting stars.

Ella blinked and shook Shaw's hand. His fingers felt as though they belonged on a building site and not in a medical facility. He didn't speak or smile, and she wondered if this couple were the doctors' version of good cop and bad cop.

Once the introductions were done, Venus took over.

'You have to understand that this place is only temporary. The portal has been unusually active recently.' She glanced at Ella. 'And we don't understand why. There are many more modern Institute facilities around the country. Doctors Shaw and Withe are in charge of all biological studies of the entities that come through that portal, and the others.'

'There are others?' Billy said.

Venus looked at Ella again. 'Yes. Didn't you know this?'

Ella ignored the question and moved forward. Then she pulled back the closest curtain to her.

She put a hand to her mouth. 'Oh, my.'

The others joined her, staring at a frail woman who must have been in her eighties lying on a bed. There was a clear tube in her arm, and when Ella followed it, she found the other end sticking into a green-skinned man with gills and webbed feet.

'I knew it,' Billy shouted. 'You're creating human-alien hybrids.'

The room went silent for a second.

Then all the adults laughed, and Venus grabbed hold of her stomach.

'My, you have a vivid imagination, Billy Beard. I think you might have been watching too many conspiracy shows on TV.'

Dr Petra Withe approached the woman on the bed and checked the machines behind her. 'I blame those ridiculous ancient aliens programmes for corrupting the minds of the nation's impressionable youth. I saw one the other night that claimed humans and dinosaurs had walked the Earth together.'

Ella ignored her words. 'What are you doing?'

Veronica Venus replied. 'Once we'd analysed the results from the interactions between the unicorn and the patients at the hospital you visited in Redcar, we tried a few other experiments. And we discovered something remarkable.'

Ella glanced at the woman sleeping on the bed.

'You discovered contact between humans and Elementals can cause healing.'

Venus stepped near to her. 'Is that what you call the creatures who come through the portals, Elementals?'

'Yes.' Ella pointed at the tube connecting the woman to the Elemental. 'What's happening there? I can't see anything moving between them. Is it supposed to be a blood transfusion?'

Dr Withe moved forward. 'There are so many things we're still in the dark about. For example, we know there is transference between the two subjects, but we're unsure what it is. It's not blood, but perhaps something invisible.'

'You're doing this to heal people?' Hannah said.

'Of course,' Venus said. She glanced at Ella. 'We're not terrible people. Come, let me show you the others.'

She took them through the rest of the room and described what was happening. There was a young girl connected to a gnome that was healing the kid's leukaemia. A woman with dementia was getting better next to a horned creature. A half-dog, half-monkey Elemental lay next to a burn victim. A leprechaun was healing a man who appeared to have been shot in the stomach.

Venus had said there were many more facilities like it across the country, and Ella's mind was full of endless possibilities.

'Why do you call them Elementals?' Dr Withe said.

Ella stared at the adults gazing at her.

Should I tell them everything? I wanted to use Elementals to heal people and the planet. So wouldn't this be the best way to do it, with the help this Institute could provide?

I can't do it on my own, can I?

'The portals you mentioned are gaps into a world where all the things we've ever believed to be myths or legends exist. I stumbled upon one last year in Saltburn. Elementals was just a name I made up.' There was the first lie. She glanced at the Elemental on a bed next to her who had claws for hands. 'I don't call them monsters because that's not what they are.'

Dr Shaw spoke for the first time. 'What about those beasts who killed and maimed dozens of people last year?'

Ella narrowed her eyes at him. 'Every living thing is true to its nature unless taught otherwise. You wouldn't call a lion, tiger, or a shark a monster because it follows its instincts, would you?'

He lifted his hand and she saw his fingers trembling. 'They are all beasts, wild and destructive, that no sensible person would allow unchecked around humans.'

The heat was simmering in Ella's veins when Veronica Venus intervened.

'We can have the philosophical discussion later. I want to hear more about how Ella got involved with these Elementals.'

Ella rubbed against the phone in her trousers. 'Maybe we should call our parents to let them know where we are?'

Venus smiled at her. 'Unfortunately, there are no communications allowed in or out of the facility. There is no internet either.' She looked at all of them. 'But your parents are aware of your situation.'

'I made a video call earlier,' Billy blurted out.

'Internal calls are permitted,' Venus said. Then she returned her focus to Ella. 'So it wasn't you who brought all those Elementals to Britain on that momentous day last year?'

'No. They must have come through one of those portals.' There was the second lie.

'It doesn't matter what we call them,' Dr Withe said. 'The important thing is these Elementals have the potential to cure all human illnesses and diseases.'

And much, much more. But should I tell them?

Ella thought about it for thirty seconds.

And then she did.

'Elementals can also fix the environment and reverse the damage done to the climate.'

She watched the faces of the adults going through their different phases of amazement. Dr Shaw glared at her, but Ella saw the excitement sparkling inside his grey eyes. Dr Withe's face lit up like fireworks in the night sky, her eyes growing wide enough to consume the whole of her head. Veronica Venus grinned at her as if Ella were the greatest birthday present she'd ever get.

And then Ella told them all about Light.

But not about the Book of All Life.

That secret she kept to herself.

For now.

Once Ella had explained about Light, Veronica Venus escorted them out of the steelworks. Shaw and Withe had got into an excited huddle, but Venus told the teenagers it was time they went home.

'I think your parents have something exciting to tell you, Ella.'

She led them to the front gate. Ella stared at her, still with a thousand questions burning inside her. She only had time for one.

'Why were your people shocking the Bigfoot with electricity?'

Venus narrowed her eyes. 'Bigfoot? Ah, yes, the big hairy chap. Well, it's like you said, Ella. Sometimes living things can't help but follow their nature. And I think travelling between worlds might fry a few brain cells. So we need to sedate anything that comes here exhibiting violent tendencies. You understand that, right? For the safety of all of our staff.'

Ella thought about it. 'Sure. So what happens next?'

Venus removed a phone from her pocket. 'You can use

this to contact me, even when I'm inside the facility.' She smiled at Ella. 'And I'll need my card back.'

Ella didn't return the smile, but swapped the VENUS card for the mobile.

'What did you mean by my parents having something exciting to tell me?'

Venus slipped the card into her jacket. 'You'll see when you get home. I wouldn't want to ruin the surprise.'

Hannah dropped gum into her mouth. 'Don't me and Bonzo get secret spy phones as well?'

Veronica Venus laughed. 'The phone I gave Ella is for all three of you.' She winked at Billy. 'I assumed you're a team. Was I wrong?'

He puffed out his cheeks. 'No. We're like the Scooby Gang.'

'Without the dog,' Hannah said as she blew a bubble. 'Or the van.'

Venus continued laughing as she waved her hand in the air, turned from them, and returned to the steelworks. Billy ran for the bikes and his bags of toys while Hannah stood with Ella.

'Well, what do you make of all that, Magic Girl?'

She ignored the jab. 'I'm not sure. I wish I could find some information about this Institute and Veronica Venus.'

Hannah slapped Ella on her back. 'I'll help you with that, my friend. It's getting late now, but if you come to Billy's tomorrow, I'll show you how to hack the world's toughest networks.'

Ella's eyes widened. 'You can do that?'

Hannah clapped her hands. 'Of course. But you'll have to leave that phone the Venus woman gave you at home.'

'Why?' Ella said.

'It's bound to have a bug in it. And I'd guess the camera

and microphone have been set to spy on you. I bet that's why she gave it to you.'

Ella removed the mobile from her pocket and stared at it. 'Won't it be doing that now and have heard what you just said?'

Hannah shook her head. 'It's not switched on.'

'Are you two coming?' Billy shouted.

They ran to him and retrieved their bikes. As Ella dragged hers over the fence, she remembered standing amongst the trees not so long ago and the ground moving towards them.

Rats. Maybe that was an omen for what we found under the steelworks.

Billy looked at her. 'Are you going to tell your parents about the Twists?'

Ella took out her phone and sent a text.

I'm on my way home.

Then she answered his question. 'What could I tell them?'

Her mobile vibrated with a new message.

That's great, love. Your father is making dinner, and we have some good news for you.

She showed it to her friends.

'Maybe they already know about your cousins,' Billy said. 'These Institute people might have told them. That could be the good news.'

Ella considered it. 'I guess I'll find out when I get home.'

Hannah smiled at her. 'Let's go then. Me and Bonzo have a longer journey than you, and I'm sure the grumbling I can hear is his stomach wanting food again.'

They turned their bikes for Redcar and set off. Ella went with the Beards all the way down the bike path along the Coast Road, turning off when they got to Marske. She watched them cycle down the back road towards Saltburn before heading home.

She kept off the roads as much as possible, focusing on her surroundings while her mind was full of what she'd seen below the steelworks. The mystery of the missing Twists had been solved, and the girls should have all the help they needed from the doctors at the Institute.

Dolly, Dotty and Daisy hated me even before Pandora forced them into being one living thing. Being together like that must have made their hate worse. I'm sure with time and the right help, they'll get better.

Ella convinced herself of that.

And if her Uncle George had stolen that money and taken Aunt Ida to South America, the police would catch up with them, eventually.

She arrived outside the house with one last thought.

With the help of Veronica Venus and the Institute, Elementals will come here to heal people and save the world.

And I won't have to do anything.

Ella put the bike in the garage and went inside to look for her parents, as happy as she'd been in a long time. The smell of roasted vegetables hit her as she ran into the living room, finding her mum and dad looking as pleased as punch.

Her mother beamed at her. 'And how was my darling daughter's adventure today?'

Do they know what happened to me at the steelworks? Has Venus really sent Institute people here to tell them everything?

Ella didn't know what to say until she remembered what was in her back pocket.

'It was good, Mum. I got this bargain at the boot sale.'

She handed it to her mother.

Gemma Finn grinned. '*The Great British Folklore and Superstition Map.*' She put it to one side. 'We'll have a look through it together later, Ella. We need to eat now before the food goes cold. Your father has been bent over a hot stove all afternoon.'

Ella didn't realise how hungry she was until she filled her plate with vegetables, pasta, and her father's favourite chilli sauce. The spices tickled her throat, and she ate as if it was her last meal on Earth.

'We've had an eventful day as well,' her mother said as she poured glasses of wine for herself and her husband. 'Would you like to hear our good news?'

Ella nodded as she slurped orange juice between her lips.

Her father wiped sauce from his chin. 'I've got a new job.'

Ella dropped her fork on to the table and gulped. 'Are we going back to London?'

Her mum and dad glanced at each other.

'Do you want to go back to London?' Gemma Finn said.

Juice and chilli bubbled around in the pit of Ella's belly.

'No... no, definitely not. I love it here.' She looked at her father. 'But I thought you wanted to make a go out of working the allotment.'

Andrew Finn laughed. 'I wish I could, love. But even with your mum helping at the school and the savings we brought from Artemis, the allotment isn't enough for the three of us to live on. So I've been looking for a job here, and today I was offered one.'

Ella gulped. 'Who by?'

Her father reached behind him and retrieved a card. Then he handed it to her.

And she read the words aloud.

'The Institute. Making science work for the community. And the world.'

Ella's fingers trembled and she dropped the card into her food.

'Hey!' her father shouted as he snatched it up. 'It's the only one I have.'

Chilli sauce stained one-third of the card as he cleaned it on a paper towel.

Ella shoved her hands under the table to stop the shaking, but it didn't work.

'Who are the Institute and what's the job?'

Andrew Finn grinned at her.

'They're a private company dedicated to improving the lives of those ignored or abandoned by governments. They've offered me a job developing local land to improve crop production. I start tomorrow.' Her expression must have told him something was worrying his daughter. 'Unless you don't want me to.'

Her mother came to her. 'When we lived in London, I know your father and I both let our work overtake our lives, all of our lives, and we didn't spend as much time with you as we should have.' Gemma glanced at her husband. 'And we'll never forgive ourselves for letting you think we'd disappeared for six months, but that will never happen again.' She took Ella's hand. 'In fact, the woman who visited today and offered your father the job even said there would be days when you could go with him to see what they do. Doesn't that sound great?'

Ella felt the warmth of her mother's skin, but it wasn't enough to stop the chill from spreading through her heart.

'This woman, was it Veronica Venus?'

Her mother shook her head. 'No. It was Kate Price. Who's Veronica Venus?'

Ella grinned. 'I'm only joking. Last year, I read a book called *The Institute*, and there was a character in it named Veronica Venus.'

Her father rubbed at his chin. 'Was it the Stephen King one? I'm not sure if you're old enough to be reading those kinds of books.'

'No, not that,' Ella said. 'It was about dragons and monsters and stuff like that.'

Gemma Finn grabbed her wine. 'Don't talk about dragons and monsters.'

Ella pressed her hands into her legs under the table. 'Why not?'

Her mother took a large drink from her glass. When she finished, Ella thought she looked like a vampire with a red stain on her lips.

'We got another one of those leaflets today. The Destroy All Monsters ones.'

Ella sighed under her breath. 'Oh, them. Just ignore their nonsense, Mum.'

'We do, love,' her father said. 'But then a group of them knocked on our door this afternoon.'

'What?' Ella's hand jerked off her leg and smacked into the table. A shiver of pain ran through her fingers before speeding up her arm.

Was it those two lads from the boot sale? How would they know where I live?

'Your dad answered while I was in the backroom reading. I left him to it until I heard raised voices and went to the door to see what was happening.'

Andrew Finn rolled his eyes. 'It was a lot of fuss about nothing, Gemma.'

Gemma Finn finished her drink. 'Not from what I saw.

They were going on about keeping the town pure and rooting out all the foreigners.'

Ella's father shook his head. 'They didn't say foreigners; they said monsters. You know, the things that don't exist.'

Her mother refilled her glass. 'Then why did you end up rolling around in the garden throwing wet punches at each other?'

Ella jolted forward and hit her elbow on the table. 'What?'

Andrew Finn waved his hand in the air. 'It was just a misunderstanding. I stepped out to tell them to leave and my foot slipped on the grass. When I tried to stop myself from falling, I pulled one of them down with me.'

Ella's mother laughed with wine on her lips. 'Ha! Is that what it was.' She stared at her daughter. 'Trust me. Those DAM people are damned loons. You, me and everyone else should stay well away from them.'

Ella nodded, and then cleared the table. After she'd filled the dishwasher, she went to her bedroom. When she got there, she took out the phone Venus had given her. She didn't turn it on.

Then she lay on her bed, staring at the ceiling and thinking about the day she'd had.

Veronica Venus had claimed the Institute was helping people get better using the Elementals who'd crossed over to this world.

And the Institute had given her father a job. A job Ella's family needed to stay living in the area.

The Institute.

Tomorrow, with Hannah's help, she'd find out who they really were.

E lla saw her father off to work the next day. He went to kiss her on the cheek, but she dodged it.

I'm far too old for that.

Instead, she asked him a question.

'Where's your office, Dad? Is it at the steelworks?'

Andrew Finn grabbed the bag containing his packed lunch and a bottle of water.

'What? No, why would it be there? The government is having that place cleaned up, and that will take a few years. The Institute has provided me with an office in the Beacon.'

Gemma Finn did kiss him. 'At least you'll have a nice view while you're working.'

'I thought you'd be out in the field, Dad.'

Andrew Finn smiled at his daughter. 'Is that a joke, love?'

Ella grinned. 'Maybe. There's a pub in the Beacon, isn't there? Is that why your office is there?'

The Redcar Beacon was sometimes called a vertical pier and stood on the seafront. Ella knew little about it until her parents bought a house in the town. In the six months she'd lived in Saltburn with her aunt and cousins, she'd never visited it. Now she saw it most days when she rode her bike along the coast.

The first time she'd ridden up to it, she was disappointed, expecting a vertical pier to reach into the clouds, but it wasn't even as tall as her school.

'They do food as well,' her father said. 'So perhaps you and your mother could meet me there one night after work for pizza?'

'Maybe,' Ella said as she watched him leave. Her mother wasn't working today, so she'd retreated into the kitchen. Ella returned to her bedroom to see if Billy had texted her.

She checked on her other mobile; the one Venus had given her. She'd taken Hannah's advice and left it switched off, but was still wary of it. Once she'd decided it was harmless, she showered and got dressed. She put the Venus phone on the side and went downstairs.

Her mother was drying pots in the kitchen.

'What are you going to do with your first day of the school holidays, love?'

Ella pursed her lips and thought of the correct answer.

I can't tell her about Billy because I'm not supposed to see him, or about Hannah since she's Billy's cousin. And I don't think she'd be happy with me hanging around with an older girl who smokes.

'I'm going to the gare to watch the ships sail by.' Of course, it wasn't a total lie as she might go there after she'd watched Hannah hack into the Institute's computer system.

Gemma Finn smiled at her daughter. 'Okay, Ella, but you be careful on that road.

'I'll be fine, Mum.'

She said goodbye to her mother and thought about the

road that ran behind the closed fence of the steelworks. And the portal under the ground.

It must have been there for years. Maybe not as big as it is now, but that's why Billy's grandfather heard and saw so many strange things: Elementals trying to cross into our world, but they couldn't because the doorway was too small then.

She stood outside and texted Billy.

Should I come over now?

Ella waited for his reply and walked to the fence separating the house from the road. There wasn't much traffic that early in the morning, but she didn't feel like riding her bike to Saltburn. Her legs ached from the day before, so she wouldn't walk there either.

Billy hadn't replied as she left the estate and headed for the bus stop.

He's probably still in bed. And I didn't get Hannah's number.

When she reached the bus stop, Ella checked the app on her phone to see when the next bus was due. It would be a ten-minute wait.

Ella sat on the bench and flicked through her mobile. The temptation to check the DAM website ran through her, but she ignored it. Her mother was right when she said the best course of action was to ignore those people.

She glanced through the other apps on her phone, surprised to see forty-six unread notifications on Myth-Maker. Ella checked them, accepting all the friend's requests without seeing who they were from. After doing that, she played the game for the first time since downloading the app.

Computer games and apps had never held much interest for her before, but it didn't take long for it to grip her. She had been on the bus for five minutes, was heading towards Saltburn when her Artemis avatar was killed.

'Damn!' she said and thumped her hand into the seat in front of her. A few of the passengers frowned at her, but she ignored them and focused on her phone. Her character in the game started out in Ancient Greece, on a quest to gather magical artefacts. The goal was to find Artemis's missing brother, Apollo. Ella's first task was a simple one: gathering berries and mushrooms from the forest to increase her strength. Unfortunately, Ella was doing this as the bus turned a corner, and, in the game, a large bird swooped down from the trees and killed her.

It annoyed her, but it was a lesson learnt. She knew to watch out for the bird on her second attempt and she dodged it easily. It flew off behind her and she continued through the forest.

Beyond that, she saw a glittering city. The details on the screen told her she had to enter it to find a magical bow and arrow. As she moved her Artemis avatar forward, she received a text from Billy.

Hannah and me finishing our pancakes. See you soon.

She was about to reply when the bus drove over something, bumping the passengers around. When Ella looked at her phone, she saw Artemis had been killed again. An ogre pointed at the screen, moving its large head and laughing at her.

Ella swore under her breath and closed the game. Then she replied to Billy.

Save me some pancakes.

Twelve minutes later, the bus arrived in the centre of Saltburn. She got off and walked to Billy's place. She went through the town, past a church, and then a fish and chip shop. It was only ten o'clock, but the smell of fried fish lingered in the air, and she tried to ignore it. Then she cut down an alley and stepped into Billy's street.

The Beard house was halfway down, a three bedroomed terrace.

She knocked on the door.

Hannah opened it and let her in. Toffee sauce was on her lips and a glint in her eyes.

'Billy's ma and pa are out, so we've got the gaff to ourselves.'

Ella followed her into the living room, the smell of pancakes tickling the insides of her stomach. A plate of them waited for her on a coffee table as Billy watched TV.

He paused the programme and smiled at her. 'I've saved you the best bits.'

She returned his grin, sat down, and grabbed a fork.

'That's why you're my friend, Billy.'

Hannah slumped into the seat next to her. 'Bonzo told me he's your only mate.'

Ella shovelled half a pancake into her mouth, speaking as she ate. 'Aren't we friends?' It tasted like the food of the gods as it slithered down her throat, all sweet and sugary.

The older teenager threw her arm around Ella's shoulder. 'Of course we are, Magic Girl. You're the most interesting person I've met in years. And now we're going to spy on this secret organisation together.'

Ella put the plate on the table. 'I'm not so sure how secret the Institute is.'

'Why?' Billy said.

She told them about her father's new job.

Hannah rubbed her chin as if she was about to investigate a crime.

'That's very coincidental.'

'I don't believe in coincidences,' Ella said. 'I checked

their website last night and, according to that, the Institute is a not-for-profit organisation run by a charitable group involved in environmental issues.'

'What's a not-for-profit organisation?' Billy said.

Hannah reached over and ruffled his hair. 'Don't you go to school, cousin?'

He squirmed out of her reach and scowled at her.

'They don't make any money for themselves, Billy,' Ella said.

'The bit your dad works for must be a front,' Billy said. 'Something the people we met yesterday can hide behind. Then they'll be able to travel all over the country, even the world, claiming to do charitable acts while running their secret missions.'

Ella and Hannah gazed at him, open-mouthed.

Then his cousin laughed. 'I guess all those conspiracy shows have taught you something useful after all.'

Ella ate more of the pancake, then spoke to Hannah.

'Does this mean you won't be able to discover what the Institute is up to?'

Hannah grabbed a laptop from the floor. 'We'll soon find out.' She flipped open the screen, and then danced her fingers over the keyboard.

Ella stared at her in amazement. 'Wow. We should call you Hannah Dancing Fingers.'

Hannah grinned at her. 'That's a good one.'

Numbers and letters skipped across the computer and mesmerised Ella.

'How does this work? Won't the police come knocking on the door in a few minutes?'

'It's all about the algorithms,' Hannah said. 'Data about cyberattacks and information theft is lurking in the dark web if you know where to look. Once you have a secret pathway, a back door, you can get into any computer system. Lazy passwords are the easiest.' She grinned at them. 'You wouldn't believe what some big, important organisations use as passwords for their network security. For example, the BBC used to have TV123 as a password for their computers.'

'No offence, Hannah, but how does a sixteen-year-old girl know all this?' Ella said.

Hannah spoke and typed at the same time. 'I've always been good with computers. Then, about five years ago, I got interested in hacking groups and learnt all I could about them online. It was another few years before I could find my way around the dark web and avoid all the scammers and nasty people. Then it was all about practice, practice, practice.'

Billy peered at the computer screen. 'So you've done this before?'

Hannah laughed. 'Once or twice. I got into the MI5 servers last year. That was interesting.'

'MI5?' Billy said.

'The British security service,' Hannah replied.

He whistled. 'I know who they are. This should be a doddle for you then.'

She grinned. 'It is since I left a hack there to get back into them. If anyone knows anything about this Institute, and not the charitable front, it would be MI5.'

Ella nodded. 'You're right. But isn't it dangerous? If you're caught, won't you lead them straight here?'

'Perhaps, but there's no excitement in life without a few risks. But it might take a while. So why don't you join Bonzo and watch one of his conspiracy shows?'

Ella stood and dragged Billy with her before he punched his cousin. Then, she took her friend into the kitchen. She glanced at the walls covered with shiny new blue and white tiles.

'Your parents have decorated since my last visit.'

He wriggled from her grasp. 'Ma moaned at me da for long enough.' He went to the sink and poured them glasses of water, handing one to her.

'Thanks,' she said.

He sipped at his and stared into the living room. 'What do you think of her?'

Ella followed his stare. 'Your cousin? I've only known her for two days, but she seems okay for a sixteen-year-old. Don't you get on with her?'

Billy placed his glass on the side. 'Yeah, I do. She's great, you know, like a sister to me. But sometimes, well, the name-calling and the punches are a bit much. I get enough of that from kids at school. I don't need it from my family.'

'You should tell her this.'

He shook his head. 'She'd only laugh at me.'

Ella moved towards him, thinking he needed a hug. And then Hannah shouted from the other room.

'I'm through.'

19 CHILDREN OF THE SUN

Billy and Ella returned to the living room. Hannah was hunched over the laptop, staring at a screen full of data.

'They've improved their security since last time, but it's no match for me.'

Her fingers danced across the keyboard as Billy sat next to her.

He clutched the glass of water in his hands. 'Have you found anything?'

She scrunched her face at him. 'I'm quick, little cousin, but give me a chance.'

Ella glanced at the TV. The sound was muted as a fake UFO crashed somewhere in America. She walked across the room, peering at the painting above the mantelpiece. A group of dogs were sitting around a table, playing cards. It was a new purchase since the last time she'd visited the house, but she'd seen it before online. She wasn't sure what it was supposed to mean. Her father had told her all paintings had hidden meanings below the surface, and she imagined a different version where an Elemental replaced each dog.

Then she had a sudden image of Pandora and Veronica Venus sitting there, gambling on the fate of the world.

Could Pandora return here using the portal we saw underneath the steelworks, or one like it?

She furrowed her eyebrows at the thought of it.

Then Ella jumped when Hannah slammed her hand on the table.

'Damn, they've got tricky since the last time.'

'No luck?' Ella said as she flicked through a stack of magazines on the sideboard.

Hannah ran her tongue over her lips. 'I've tried searching for any mentions of the Institute, but got nothing.'

Ella sighed, knowing she'd got her hopes up too high with this. She stared at the cover of a glossy magazine, looking into the eyes of someone who had died over fifty years ago. Then she read the headline aloud.

'*The JFK Conspiracy Continues.*' She returned it to the pile of similar mags. 'Are these yours, Billy?'

He shook his head. 'They're me da's. He loves that kind of stuff.'

'It's more like guff than stuff,' Hannah said as she thumped the keyboard.

Ella rejoined her on the sofa. 'Maybe you should stop before you get caught. It doesn't look like there's anything there, anyway.'

Hannah puffed out her cheeks. 'But there must be. You can't have a super-secret organisation running around the country collecting mythological creatures without the British security services knowing. It's impossible.'

Ella stretched her legs. 'You said it yourself, Hannah. So

if it's super-secret, the information is probably hidden some-where else.'

'Or you're not looking in the right way,' Billy said.

The girls turned to him.

Hannah furrowed her eyebrows. 'What do you mean, little cousin?'

He grinned. 'Well, if it were me, I wouldn't call it the Institute when adding secret stuff into the computer. Instead, I'd give it a codename, just like I would with any other group.'

Hannah lifted her hand and Ella thought she was going to punch him. But she put her arm around his shoulder and hugged him.

'You are a super spy.' She smiled at him. 'And my favourite cousin.'

While his cheeks changed to a delicate shade of pink, Hannah returned to the computer. It wasn't long before she found what she wanted.

'Billy was right.' She pointed at the screen. 'Look at this.'

Ella leant over and read what was on the laptop.

'IG1 to IG12. What does that mean?'

'Institute Group 1 to Institute Group 12,' Hannah said. 'They're super lazy at MI5 because IG was the first code I tried.' She grinned at Ella. 'Do you want to see what's behind these links?'

Ella answered by grabbing the computer and using her finger to place the pointer over IG1.

Then she clicked.

Information unrolled across the screen, a vast amount of data and links, with the first line appearing to be the date the Institute was formed. And by whom.

Billy whistled. 'Created in 1926 by Winston Churchill.'

Ella stared at the dates on the first line. '1926 to 1939.' Then she clicked on IG2. '1939 to 1945.' Then IG12. '2001 to now.'

She scanned through them all; they were in sections of dates, all of various lengths. Ella scrolled down the list of data, seeing dates and labels for events. She clicked on the one for March 1998, London, and read the description.

'Sightings of a winged creature seen flying over Kings Cross. Twenty-five witness reports. Photographs and videos are in the attached folder.'

This was listed below and she opened it. She went past the images and selected the first video. It showed a busy area outside the train station, a place Ella had visited countless times when she'd lived in London. She'd seen many unusual things there, but nothing like what appeared in the clip; it resembled a small whale, grey in colour, with vast wings flapping as if its life depended upon it. Then, it swooped down at the people standing there, letting out a shriek that hurt Ella's ears.

As well as its awful howl, she heard the screams and cries of the crowd. Some of them ran away, while others appeared frozen in shock. The Elemental, for that's what it must have been, terrorised the area for a minute before a group of brave souls chased it off. But from what Ella saw, nobody seemed injured.

She returned to the previous screen and read how the Institute, through the government, had reported the creature as an advertising stunt for a movie filmed in London. Next, she went back and located the entry for 2 June last year. When she opened it, there was a list of events on that day across Great Britain. She found the entries for Saltburn and looked through them. There was no mention of her or the Twists. Still, they included eyewitness accounts of the Elementals Ella had brought over to repair the environment: the flying horses, the mermaids, and the gnomes.

Then she scanned the reports for the incidents in Carlisle, Dublin, Dundee, and Humberside. She couldn't read too much, with the ache in her heart increasing every time she read about Elementals attacking and killing people.

Pandora did that, but how much was my responsibility as well?

Hannah snatched the laptop from Ella.

'All this shows is the Institute has been following strange events for nearly a century. It doesn't tell us if we should trust them or not.'

Ella sank into the sofa, unsure of how she felt.

If they can help me bring Elementals here to fix the climate and give Dad a job, what's there to worry about?

'Can you look for something for me?' Billy said.

Hannah shrugged. 'Sure, cousin. What are you after?'

He took a deep breath. 'I know you keep laughing at me about aliens, but I want to know what happened at Rendlesham Forest in 1980.'

Ella shook her head. 'Is this one of your conspiracy theories?'

He frowned at her. 'It's the most famous UFO event to have occurred in the United Kingdom and is among the best-known reported UFO events worldwide. So it's Britain's Roswell.'

Hannah pursed her lips. 'Are we supposed to know what that is?'

'A UFO crashed in Roswell, New Mexico, in 1947, and

the American government covered it up. Just like our politicians covered up that event at Kings Cross.'

'So you think a UFO crashed in this forest in 1980?' Ella said.

Billy's eyes lit up. 'No. It didn't crash, but flew in and out of the forest over three days. There are several witnesses to this, including people from the nearby American air force base. One officer even recorded his observations on tape.' He pointed at the laptop. 'See if it's mentioned in those IG files.'

Hannah tutted, but still clicked on the IG11 link. When it opened, the list showed reported incidents from 1980 to 2001.

And the first one was Rendlesham Forest.

'Blimey,' Ella said.

Billy clapped his hands. 'I told you.' Then he read out the details. 'A large glowing triangle was seen floating in the forest. When servicemen from the base tried to approach it, the object floated away from them, but not out of sight. Some claimed to have heard strange noises coming from the thing. The phenomenon was observed over three consecutive nights.'

Ella peered at the information on the screen as Billy finished reading. 'It could have been a portal into the Elemental world, like the one under the steelworks.'

He grinned at her. 'Do you believe me now?'

Ella didn't know what to believe anymore. From what she'd seen over the last few days, Elementals had been coming to Earth for at least a hundred years, and the British government had known about it all this time.

And the Institute had been a big part of that.

Which means they have the experience to help me.

Hannah leant over her cousin's shoulder. 'These reports from Rendlesham cover three days, from various military personnel.'

'So?' Billy said.

She turned to Ella. 'This isn't like what we saw under the steelworks. That portal was static. The lights people saw moved around, rose in the air, and then disappeared.'

Ella considered what she'd said. 'That was over thirty years ago and in a different place. Maybe the gaps between the Elemental world and ours fluctuated more then. Unfortunately, the damage to the climate has got a lot worse as well.'

'Don't you think it was a UFO?' Hannah said.

Billy snorted his answer but, didn't talk. Ella did.

'I know little about UFO sightings, but many of them are people seeing lights in the sky. That sounds like a portal to another world to me.'

'What about the Greys?' Billy said.

'Who?' Ella replied.

Billy stood, holding out his arms as if about to give a speech.

'The Greys are aliens, human-like with small bodies and smooth grey-coloured skin; enlarged hairless heads; and large black eyes. Loads of people have seen them over the years. They've even abducted people.'

Ella thought she should start taking what he was saying seriously.

'They sound as if they could be Elementals. The idea they've abducted people is worrying.'

Billy nodded. 'And scary.'

Ella agreed. 'Why would they do that?'

Billy's eyes lit up. 'Experiments. They want to create alien-human hybrids.'

Hannah grimaced. 'That sounds terrible.' She grabbed him around the shoulder. 'You better watch out, little cousin, that some monster girl doesn't grab you for her boyfriend.'

They laughed together as Ella stared at the computer screen.

'We'll have to ask Veronica Venus about all of this.'

Hannah let go of Billy. 'Do you trust her?'

Ella shrugged. 'I guess we have to for now.' She pointed at the laptop. 'Should you log out of that in case they discover you?'

Hannah agreed. 'That's a good idea.' She danced her fingers across the keyboard and closed everything in a flash. Then she pushed the computer to the side and stretched her legs over the table. 'What do we do next?'

Ella scratched at the itch in her palm. 'I go home and turn on the phone Venus gave me.'

'Will you tell her about the Book of All Life?' Billy said.

Should I do that?

She got off the sofa. 'If we're going to fix the environment, then I suppose I should. If the Institute has over a hundred years' experience of dealing with Elementals, having the book can only help them.'

'But only you can use it?' Hannah said.

Ella nodded. 'Yes.'

Billy grinned at her. 'That means you'll become an agent for the Institute.' His smile lit up the room. 'Maybe we all will.'

He danced around the sofa as if he was at a disco. His happiness was infectious and Ella beamed at him.

'Perhaps things are finally working out for us.'

Then she glanced at the TV screen and saw the emergency news broadcast.

There were reports of a major incident happening in the UK.

In the northeast of England.

In Redcar.

At the Beacon.

20 PURPLE HAZE

Ella threw herself across the table, knocking the laptop to the floor. She grabbed the TV remote and turned the sound on. She sat there with Billy and Hannah and listened to the news report.

'Information is reaching us of an attack in Redcar. Eyewitnesses are reporting seeing people fleeing the Beacon building. The police have cordoned off the area and closed the roads around the incident.'

Then the camera switched to the scene, focusing on the tall structure where Ella's father had gone to work only a few hours ago. There appeared to be smoke rising from the top of it. Ella clutched at her chest, expecting the place to burst into flames at any second. She wanted to tear her gaze from the sight, but couldn't.

She reached into her pocket for her phone, dialling her father's number while still watching the screen. As it rang, she saw the smoke drift from the building and move slowly to the ground. The police appeared to have moved most of the public away, but a few were still there, unfazed by what was approaching them.

Hannah pointed at the TV. 'That smoke is purple.'

Ella peered at it, and so did the people on the street. The police had their backs to the smoke, but turned when someone must have said something to them.

Then the smoke settled on all of them.

And they grabbed at their throats before dropping to the ground.

'Jesus!' Billy said.

The cameras lingered on the scene for twenty seconds before cutting back to the female news presenter. The shock on her face was replicated in Ella's heart.

'I'm sorry, we cut out there. We'll return to it as soon as we can.'

Ella turned from the screen to look at her phone, watching it ringing with no answer. She stared at it for an eternity before ending the call. When she looked at the TV, all it was showing was a frozen image of the purple smoke drifting out of the Beacon.

The three of them sat there in stunned silence, gazing at the image.

Then Ella stood. 'I've got to go there.' The mobile shook in her trembling fingers.

'It's too dangerous,' Billy said. 'We should let the police deal with it until we know what's going on with that smoke.'

'No,' Ella said. 'I can't leave my dad in there. I have to get inside that building.'

'How?' Billy said.

Ella lifted the phone to her chest. 'I'll call a taxi, have the driver take me as close as possible to the Beacon.'

Hannah stood next to her. 'There's no need for that. I'll drive.'

Ella looked at her. 'You have a car?'

Hannah shook her head. 'No. I'll take Aunt Chloe's.'

'What?' Billy said. 'Me ma won't be happy about that.'

His cousin went to the bookcase and picked up the car keys from the middle shelf.

'She'll never know, Billy.' She pointed the keys at him. 'Unless you tell her.'

Ella tried not to think about what might have happened to her father.

'You know how to drive?'

'Since I was twelve.' Hannah moved forward. 'Are we going?'

Ella followed her out and Billy locked the door behind them. The pain in Ella's heart was growing by the second as she struggled to control her breathing. She closed her eyes and opened them again, hoping that would wipe away the image of those people collapsing when the purple smoke settled on them. But it didn't. Finally, she focused on Hannah standing next to a small orange car. Ella got into the front, with Billy in the back.

He leant in to them. 'Are you sure about this, Ella?'

Her lips trembled as she spoke. 'I have to find out what's going on.'

Hannah inserted the keys and started the engine. 'I'll take the quickest route and get us as close as possible.'

Ella didn't reply. She was still holding her mobile, too worried to call her father's number again.

Should I call Mum and see how she is?

They left Saltburn as she considered that question.

No. I don't want to worry her until I know what's happened at the Beacon.

What she did was use her phone to check online for news about the incident. There were very few genuine details from the leading news sites, but dozens of posts spreading gossip and conspiracy theories. She skipped through a few and discovered they all mentioned the same thing.

The monsters are attacking us.

She went on Twitter, looking for the latest comments. There were hundreds of them, mainly from other parts of the country. But there were a few from Redcar, and when Ella read them, she saw they all followed the same theme.

DAM were right, we're under attack.

Purple smoke monsters killing people in Redcar. DAM will protect you. Don't trust the police.

There were several links to the DAM website and she clicked on the top one. Her heart froze at the images, photos of the bodies on the ground with their faces all twisted out of shape. And their skin was purple.

FEAR RIPPLED through her as she stared at the screen, wondering if that was what her father looked like inside the Beacon.

He's fine. I have to believe that.

Ella put the phone away and gazed out of the window. She might not have the power the Light gave her anymore, but she had enough experience dealing with the unusual to trust she could handle what was happening at the Beacon.

And that she could help her father and anyone else trapped inside that building.

I need to stay calm.

She focused on the road, watching the car pass through Marske and on to the Coast Road. Billy was quiet in the back while Hannah concentrated on her driving.

Ella closed her eyes, seeing the purple smoke drifting from the Beacon and attacking those people again.

It wasn't an accident. The smoke selected those people.

Is that what happened to Dad?

'They've shut the road into Redcar,' Hannah said.

Ella opened her eyes to see the flashing lights ahead of them.

'Pull over and park outside the houses on the left. I know how to get there.'

Hannah did that. As they got out of the car, there were crowds on both sides of the road, many of whom were pointing into the sky. Ella looked up and saw the helicopters above the town as if it was a scene from a war movie. She heard them buzzing above her like angry bees, watching as they headed towards the Beacon.

'What are we going to do now?' Billy said.

Ella put a hand on his shoulder. 'You and Hannah are staying here. I can't let you risk your lives by coming with me.'

He peered into her eyes. 'We're not leaving you.'

Hannah nodded. 'The squirt is right. We're a team now. Whatever happens to you happens to all of us.' She glanced at the activity in the sky. 'So how are we going to get to the Beacon with everywhere closed off?'

'Not everywhere.' Ella watched the helicopters moving above the town. 'Those choppers look like they're only focused on the Beacon and the High Street. And that means they've left one important bit free.'

'Where?' Hannah said.

Ella pointed at the sea. 'The beach.'

She ran across the road. Billy and Hannah followed her as the noise in the sky increased, as if a thousand locusts flew above them. She got to the beach first before moving to the large wall built as a sea defence. Her heart was beating fast enough to power the windmills she saw standing in the ocean.

She placed her hand on the concrete, feeling wet sand there.

Then Billy joined her. 'If one of those copters turns around, they'll see us out in the open like this.'

She peered into the sky and knew he was right.

'It's a risk we'll have to take. If we stick to the wall, it will lead us to the Beacon, and there's a way into the building from the beach.'

'What about that purple smoke?' Hannah said.

Ella peered at her. 'Hopefully, it'll have gone by then.'

Do I really believe that?

The three of them looked at each other for a second before Ella turned and led them towards the Beacon. She concentrated on what was in front of her, thinking about what she'd do when they reached their destination. The smell of the sea drifted into her head as gulls squawked above her. There was no conversation between them, but Ella was glad the others were with her.

But I won't let them go into the Beacon with me. Whatever is in there, I need to face it alone.

They ran at a steady pace, dodging bits of rubbish and randomly dropped chips on the route. The buzzing continued in the sky, but she didn't look up, reluctant to find a helicopter peering back at her. The thump in her heart matched the noise above her head, punching against her ribs like an angry man trying to smash his way out of a prison cell.

Drifting sea fret settled on her face and crawled between her lips. She tasted the saltwater as it slipped down her throat, hoping it might fill the gaping hole growing inside her gut. She ran her fingers across the sea wall as she went, wanting its concrete touch to give her the strength Ella knew she'd need when she reached her destination.

After five minutes, she saw the steps leading to the Beacon, her heart rate increasing by the second. Her leg muscles flexed as she pounded her feet over the stone. She turned her hands into fists, ready for anything.

Until two police officers stepped in front of her and she fell to the ground.

She bounced off the concrete and tumbled down the steps, ending up in a heap in the sand. Ella rolled to the side, a jolt of pain zipping through her hip as blood trickled from her fingers.

'You kids shouldn't be here,' a policewoman said as she reached down to help Ella up.

As she stood, Ella saw the other copper escorting Billy and Hannah off the beach. The policewoman let go of her hand and nodded for Ella to follow her friends.

But she didn't move. 'What's happened inside the Beacon?'

The woman shook her head. 'I don't know, kid. But nobody can go near it. We're waiting for the army to arrive. Now come on, I need to get you out of here.'

Ella stood still. 'My father is in that building.'

'I'm sorry, kid, but I'm sure he wouldn't want you putting yourself in harm's way, would he?'

Ella knew the officer was right, but frustration swept through her. She climbed the steps, reaching the top to see Hannah and Billy taken into the back of a police car. Then she stared at the Beacon, seeing no purple smoke anywhere and wondering if her father was inside the building.

Then she saw a familiar face.

She ran towards DS Keita. 'Dominique,' she shouted.

DS Keita turned from her uniformed colleagues. 'Ella, you shouldn't be here.'

'My dad's in there.' She pointed at the Beacon. 'I have to get in to help him.'

DS Keita pulled Ella away from the road. 'We don't have your father on the list of employees in the building.'

Ella twisted out of the police officer's grasp. 'He only started working there today.'

'Okay,' DS Keita said. 'But you still need to leave the scene.'

'What's going to happen, Dominique?'

DS Keita sighed. 'We're waiting for specialist officers to arrive.'

As she said that, two large trucks came towards them from the other end of the town, moving past the cinema. DS Keita turned to glance at them.

It was the fraction of a second Ella needed.

She pulled away from Dominique and ran for the Beacon.

Then she went inside.

21 THE BEACON

bove the noise of the gulls squawking near her head, Ella heard Dominique screaming at her. She ignored everything and sprinted inside the Beacon. The place smelt as if it needed a good clean, with an aroma of rotten fish lingering everywhere. The stink distracted her from the damp at her feet until she looked down to see there was water leaking from under the toilet door.

As well as the entrance, there were six floors above her. The lift was open and inviting, but Ella knew she wouldn't take it.

I'd be a sitting duck if I got trapped in there.

She wasn't sure where her dad was supposed to be working, so she'd have to check everywhere using the stairs. As she thought about that, Ella heard more noises coming from outside. She turned to see DS Keita move to the side as people in uniforms jumped out of two trucks. Dominique pointed at the Beacon as ice ran down Ella's back. She could imagine what the policewoman was saying to the new arrivals and knew it wouldn't be good.

Then she heard something else.

'Ella, I'm waiting for you in here.'

The chill on her spine turned into an iceberg and sped across the whole of her body. Her fingers stiffened as her legs froze. She bit into her top lip and tasted her blood, letting the warmth slip into her mouth and bring life back into her cold flesh.

Ella forced herself forward and entered the bar opposite. The smell of fish had disappeared, replaced by the stink of burnt pizza. All the tables and chairs had been turned over as if a tornado had swept through the room. Untouched drinks stood on the bar next to a full plate of chips covered in tomato ketchup.

She moved towards it, her hand ready to take a chip when she realised the smell wasn't of tomato sauce.

It was blood.

She jerked her fingers away, stumbling back and into a table behind her. The wood stabbed into her hip as she turned to glance through the window, seeing the calmness of the sea. A seagull hovered there, unmoving as if some wondrous artist had painted it over the sky. Its gaze fixed on her with shimmering green eyes digging deep into her soul.

'Not here, Ella. Go upstairs to find what you want.'

The voice came from behind her. She turned to follow it, leaving the bar and heading up. She clung to the bannister as she went, checking everything around her. The cold rising from the ground made her glance down at the wispy purple smoke drifting at her feet.

'Don't worry, Ella, that won't hurt you.'

Her legs moved in slow motion as she continued up, moving past the rooms containing the local radio station. Then, against her better judgement, she lingered outside the window, peering through to see bodies on the floor.

The voice laughed around her.

'Go inside, Ella. You can play whatever music you want, and I'll broadcast it across the region.'

The laugh came out of the smoke and covered her like a blanket, making her flesh crawl as the voice spoke to her again.

'I'll take requests. What would you like? What about *Billy Don't Be A Hero* or *Sweet Child O' Mine?*'

Ella grimaced as she continued upstairs. 'I hate that song.'

The thing inside the smoke laughed once more. 'Good girl, so do I. But we need a tune celebrating fathers and daughters for this special occasion. So perhaps I'll play *Isn't She Lovely* by Stevie Wonder. Yes, I think Andrew Finn would like that for his daughter.'

Ella reached the top, gazing at the smoke swirling around her feet.

'Who are you?'

'You'll find out soon, once you're inside.'

She hesitated before putting her hand on the door. The wood was like ice and the chill on her spine was large enough to sink the *Titanic*. Ella pushed it open, shivering as it creaked and the sound drilled into her ears.

Ella stood in the doorway, seeing tables, chairs, and computers in what appeared to be a typical office. The smoke lifted from her feet and moved towards the window, obscuring the view of the sea.

At least I don't have to see any more demonic seagulls.

She saw a desk and the framed photos on it: one of her parents standing outside the London Eye and the other of Ella and her father smiling as they were about to descend from the top of a rollercoaster.

She wanted to pick up that photo, but her gaze was drawn to something moving inside the light shimmer of purple smoke on the floor. The haze lifted up and down as if it was lungs breathing slowly, and she heard the wheeze coming from it. Shards of electricity stabbed into every inch of her as pinpricks of red peered out of the smoke. She saw two at first, but then they multiplied to be four, and then eight, with all of them staring at her.

Ella moved back, bumping into a table and knocking papers everywhere. Before they disappeared into the mist, she noticed the top one was addressed to her father.

Dear Andrew,

Welcome to The Institute. I hope this is only the start of a great future for you and your family with us.

It sank below the purple before she could read the rest.

Then the shimmering red pinpricks turned into pairs of eyes inside twisted hairy faces that crawled out of the smoke and glared at her.

Four little creatures resembling crazed squirrels inched forward. She pushed a hand behind her, finding a desk and feeling for a weapon. Small inconsequential objects squirmed through her fingers as she never took her gaze from the things crawling forward.

'Do you like my pets, Ella? I think they love you.'

Ella searched for where the voice was coming from while scrambling her hand across the desk. She brushed a computer mouse to the side, feeling through paper clips, touching a cup until she found something useful.

She grabbed the scissors and thrust them in front of her.

'I don't want to hurt anyone. Just tell me where my father is.'

The voice laughed so hard it pushed the smoke from the floor and Ella saw the creatures in their full malevolence. They were standing straight on two legs with bony arms outstretched towards her. Their eyes bulged as if about to burst, pulsing yellow and red. When she stared at their bodies, she saw things crawling through their fur: eight-legged insects with wings on their backs.

'Your father is right here, Ella. Can't you see him?'

She kept her gaze on the murderous animals while glancing at the back of the room. The purple smoke disappeared and she saw the filing cabinets near the far wall.

Then he stepped from behind them.

Her father.

'Dad!' she shouted, ready to run to him if only those vile things weren't between them.

Andrew Finn held his hands out to his daughter.

'Hello, love. Come and give me a big kiss.'

She was about to ignore the crazed squirrels and the squirming insects coming from their fur and sprint to her father.

Until she stopped herself.

No. That's not Dad.

She gripped the scissors. 'What have you done to him?'

As Ella continued to stare at the thing that wasn't her father, she noticed the shining circle of light in the wall behind him.

It's a portal. That's how these things got here.

Andrew Finn grinned at her and she saw his face wriggle as something squirmed beneath his skin.

'This is your father, Ella. I'm only borrowing his flesh for a bit so I can visit you. I tried to contact you before, but the animals and insects of this world are too dumb to control.'

Ella's fingers moved up the scissors from the handle and across the blade. Trickles of her blood settled into her palm, the only warmth she could feel in the whole of the room.

'Why?' A heavy weight possessed her chest. 'Why have you done this?'

He went to the desk and sat on it. Purple smoke lingered around his body as the demented squirrels rubbed against his legs.

'You banished the Goddess to the outer realms. She was the only protector we had against the Kraken. You have to pay for that.'

Ella kept the scissors pointed at the creatures.

'The Kraken? That's a mythical sea monster.'

Water slipped out of her father's mouth as he spoke. 'The Kraken is a human-octopus hybrid, ten feet tall with eight giant tentacles springing from its back. Its appetite voracious, it devours any living thing in its way. Only Pandora could stop it. So she imprisoned it deep underground, but when the Goddess never returned to our realm – all because of you – the Kraken escaped and now terrorises my people.'

Ella tried not to look at how her father's skin moved on his face. She had to keep him talking while she thought of a way of saving him.

'Who are your people?'

'We are the Lorelei who were many, but now are few. The Kraken murders women and children every day, and their blood is on your hands, Ella Finn. Because of that, your family has to pay.'

She took a deep breath. 'Okay, but take me and leave my father alone.'

'Why should we do that?'

Ella fell to her knees. 'Because I'm begging you.'

Purple glowed out of her father as he moved towards her. The room smelled of the sea as Ella dug her fingers into the floor. Thick ruby-coloured veins throbbed on her father's face as if the blood was about to burst from his head.

'Good, beg some more.'

One creature was near her head, with an insect on its nose looking at her. Its mandibles twitched as saliva dripped from its mouth.

Ella closed her eyes. 'I'll give you anything you want. Just leave him alone.'

She could sense the insect close to her, knowing its hairy legs were inches from her skin. But that wasn't what was worrying her. All she saw in her mind was Ratter's grave in the garden.

An Elemental possessed Ratter's body, and not long after, the poor girl died. What if that happens to Dad?

She opened her eyes to see insects covering the demented squirrel's head. Ella couldn't stop looking at them as the Lorelei spoke through her father.

'You must return with me to my realm. Your fate will be decided there.'

'And you'll let my father go?'

The thing that wasn't Andrew Finn grinned at her.

'This meatflesh will die in my world. I'll leave it here if you promise to come with me.'

Ella knew she had no choice. 'I promise to go with you if you release him.'

She was waiting for the Elemental to reply when someone spoke behind her.

'Leave the girl alone.'

Ella jerked her head away from the insects, turning to see Veronica Venus standing in the doorway, clutching a strange-looking gun.

Before Ella could do anything, two of the demented squirrels jumped at Venus. The woman from the Institute snatched the weapon up, holding out the chunky rifle and firing at the creatures.

A loud echo boomed around the room and into Ella's ears. She grabbed her head as a yellow pulse fried the insects and they fell to the floor. They writhed on the carpet, letting out unholy screams that made Ella want to throw up. Instead, she watched Veronica Venus moving towards her.

'Stop,' Ella said.

'It's okay,' Venus said. 'My people are here now.' She glanced at Andrew Finn. 'Whatever this is, it can't hurt you.'

Then Ella's father smashed his fist into the desk.

'Are you sure about that, Institute woman?'

Ella got up, her legs trembling under her. She watched the blood leak from her father's fingers and felt the red dampness in her hand.

'You know who I am?' Venus said to Andrew Finn.

'I know what you've been doing to the unfortunate Elementals who stumble into your world.' Her father looked at Ella. 'Does she?'

Veronica Venus ignored the question and reached a hand out to Ella.

'Come on. We have to leave now.'

'No,' Ella said. 'I have to save my father, and the only way I can do that is by going through there.' She pointed at the shimmering yellow circle in the wall.

'A portal?' Venus said. 'Why would you enter that, Ella?'

'My daughter has a blood debt to pay,' Andrew Finn said.

Venus turned her back on him. 'Don't listen to that, Ella. We'll help your father at the Institute.'

Ella stared at the Institute woman.

Can I take that risk?

She thought about it for fewer than five seconds. Then she held her hand out to Venus.

'Give me your weapon. I'll return it to you when I get back.'

Ella watched Venus scrutinise her as if she was a teacher who'd just learnt Ella had been cheating in her exams.

Then she handed her the gun.

'Be careful with it. It's an experimental prototype and the only one we have.'

Ella took it, surprised by how light it was.

Then Venus whispered to her as Andrew Finn jumped off the desk.

'Okay.' He shivered as he looked at Ella, and she saw those things wriggling below his skin again. 'I'll be glad to get away from this miserable place. It's far too cold here.'

He walked to the portal and climbed through it.

Ella smiled at Veronica Venus.

Then she did the same.

22 PANDORA'S WORLD

A kaleidoscope of light shimmered around Ella. All the colours of the rainbow bombarded her eyes as she raised her hands to her face for protection. Bells and whistles exploded inside her ears and burrowed their way into her brain. A thousand distorted electric guitars used the sides of her skull as amplifiers as she kept on falling.

The back of her throat became stretched to the point she thought her tonsils were trying to tunnel out of her mouth. Her fingers shivered as she moved them from her face. The frenzied rainbow had vanished, replaced by a tiny pinprick of yellow below her.

Air whooshed around her legs as she dropped towards the light, wind rushing up and blowing the hair above her head as if she was inside a giant hairdryer. Her skin trembled and her eyebrows fluttered as she continued to fall.

A coughing fit possessed her lungs as she headed for the illumination, clutching at her throat as she reached it. Then, finally, her legs pierced it, and a warm sensation like being in hot water engulfed her.

Then the light disappeared and she fell ten feet to the

ground. There was enough time for her to brace for the landing, bending her knees before she hit the grass and rolled into a ball.

Ella tumbled through thick chunks of green, the fragrances of nature careering into her nose as she leapt up: she smelt the remains of raindrops, leaf buds, wet twigs, tree sap, bark, mossy earth, and a hint of rose bushes. She spat the last of the cough from her lungs as she scrutinised where she was. A vast, clear blue sea lay ahead while fields of grass and flowers surrounded her. To Ella's right was a never-ending forest of giant trees reaching into the sky.

She dusted herself down and looked for the gun Veronica Venus had given her.

I bet it's useless, anyway. Just because it fried a few mad squirrels and insects doesn't mean it will be any good here.

Still, she felt better when she saw it between a bunch of vivid orange and yellow flowers. She plucked it from them and held it in her hands. Ella knew nothing about guns apart from what she'd seen in movies and TV shows, but she guessed this one wasn't normal. She remembered reading a book last year, some American thriller, where the author had spent two pages describing the ins and outs of a gun. It had bored her so much she'd stopped reading, but she'd learnt that firing a gun or a rifle would have a massive effect on her.

It's the recoil when the force of the shot reflects on the shooter.

So she knew she had to be careful with the Institute rifle. Even with her limited knowledge of weapons, she thought it looked as if it had been changed beyond something the military would use. However, it was light to pick up, and she could hold it in one hand. She wasn't sure if it would work against the Elementals in this world, but without her Light, she was glad to have it.

Ella gripped the gun as she scanned her surroundings, looking for her father or the thing that had possessed him. The trees swayed in the distance and it seemed as if they were whispering to her. But it wasn't the voice she'd heard coming from the purple smoke back at the Beacon. That had come from her father. Now it was female and its owner strode towards her through the grass.

'I don't think that gun will help you here, Ella Finn.'

The woman was tall - taller than Ella's mother who was six foot without shoes - with an air of majesty surrounding her. She wore a short sleeveless blue dress. Tattoos covered her arms and legs while her long, dark hair rested on her shoulders.

Ella stood firm with the gun resting against her leg.

'If you've hurt my father, I'll kill you.'

The woman moved towards her.

'Relax, he's fine. I left his meatsack in your world. My name is Lore. Are you ready to kill the Kraken?'

Ella stared beyond her towards the sea. 'Are you human?'

Lore turned her head to the side and Ella saw the gills on her throat.

'What do you think?'

'What type of Elemental are you?'

'I told you on Earth, Ella, we are the Lorelei, banished to this realm many millennia ago. But we were happy here until you stopped the Goddess from returning to her world. We lost our protection and it's all your fault.'

Ella glanced across the grass to the sea. 'Where am I?'

Lore held up her arms and Ella saw the tattoos moving over her skin.

'This is the Banishment, the place you humans sent the Goddess and all the Elementals to thousands of years ago.'

Ella gripped the gun. 'So this is Pandora's realm, where she ruled over everything?'

'It is. Everything was fine here until you invited her back to Earth.'

Ella gritted her teeth. 'That's a lie. She tricked me into letting her go there.'

'And then you stranded her at the end of the multiverse.'

'I had no choice.'

'So you say, but you left this realm unguarded against the worst of its residents.' Lore looked across the ocean. 'And the Kraken has caused death and destruction here ever since. And that's all down to you.'

Ella had had enough of listening to the blame game.

'I'm not responsible for what happened here. Once Pandora didn't return, why didn't the Kraken follow her to Earth using the portal you brought me through?'

Lore laughed at her. 'Several Elementals have stepped through portals back to Earth, but most refuse that temptation.'

'Why?' Ella said.

'Why? Because your planet is much more dangerous than this realm, child. Even the strongest of Elementals would find themselves hunted, tortured and killed by the humans.' She held up one hand and moved it across the sky. 'Pandora always wanted to return to those who'd betrayed her, but most of the rest of us knew it was far too hazardous a place to live. There was peace here amongst the many inhabitants, kept by the Goddess, but once Pandora left, the worst of the predators took over.'

'Like the Kraken.'

Lore let out a long sigh. 'That creature is the predator king in this part of the realm.' She peered at Ella. 'I went to Earth to make you pay for this crime, but perhaps you and your human weapon will redeem yourself this day.'

Ella lifted the gun to her face. 'You said this wouldn't help me.'

'Let's hope I'm wrong.'

Ella hoped so, too. 'Where is this Kraken?'

Lore pointed to the trees. 'I'll take you to the village to meet my people. Once there, you can prepare for your battle with the great beast.'

Ella peered at Lore's gills, which moved when she spoke.

'Don't you live in the ocean?'

'The Lorelei inhabit both the land and the sea. But, unfortunately, so does the Kraken, and that's why we have no escape from it.'

She turned and strode towards the vast forest. Ella hesitated for a second, glancing at the shimmering yellow portal ten feet above her head.

I could go home now if I could reach that thing.

She dismissed the thought of leaving.

I made a promise and I won't break it, no matter how dangerous it might be here.

She ran through the long grass and caught up with Lore.

'When I've finished here, how will I reach the portal in the sky to get back home?'

Lore spoke as she walked. 'I admire your confidence, but perhaps you should concentrate on the battle awaiting you.'

Ella did that as she sucked up the sensations of this new world. Strange blue birds flew over her head while unknown buzzing insects flitted in and out of the brightly coloured flowers around them. The gun felt comfortable in her grasp and that bothered her.

I don't want to get used to using weapons like this.

And why did the Institute have it in the first place? Veronica Venus had said it was a prototype, which meant they would make more. For what? To kill Elementals?

At the steelworks, Venus had said they were only trying to help Elementals.

Then Ella remembered those things in the office, the demented looking squirrels and those awful insects.

When I had Light, I could protect myself, but it's not the same now for me and others like Veronica.

So she understood why the Institute had built such a gun. And maybe it would help her with the Kraken.

But not to kill it.

Not unless she had to.

That terrible thought echoed inside her head as they reached the edge of the forest.

Lore turned to her. 'You'll see some strange things here, but don't be too quick to use that weapon in your hand. Nothing will harm you while you're with me.'

Ella placed the gun next to her leg. 'I promise I won't.'

Lore smiled at her. 'You humans and your promises. Do you keep yours, Ella, or are you, like all the others, quick to cheat and lie to get what you want?'

Ella frowned. 'I don't lie.'

And then she thought of what she'd done to her parents, twisting their memories into untruths. And how she'd lied to the police.

'We'll see,' Lore said as she stepped into the trees.

Ella followed her in. Broken branches lay scattered across the ground. She touched one of them, feeling the damp wood on her skin. Most of them appeared to be wet, as if they'd fallen in storms long forgotten.

Brittle bark dripped from her fingers. 'It must have rained a lot recently.'

Lore plucked a vibrant green leaf from a tree.

'The seasons have been harsh since Pandora left, stripping away the bark and outer layers, yet rendering them even more beautiful.'

Ella nodded in agreement, gazing at the saplings as she dodged the debris on the ground. The trees had the appearance of driftwood, twisting in patterns that reminded her of seaside waves and of being back on the beach at Saltburn.

'Is my dad okay?'

Lore sniffed at the air and Ella noticed again the tattoos appeared to be alive on her skin.

'Andrew Finn is fine.' She stopped and turned to Ella. 'It wasn't only his body we shared, but our minds. Would you like to know what he thinks of you?'

Ella stumbled, putting her hand against a tree. The bark was soft, damp, yet her fingers came away dry.

'What? No, I don't want to know what's in his head.'

Lore laughed. 'Don't worry, it was all good. There was no bad there, only love and all the positive things he thinks about you. Although...'

She turned from Ella and started walking again.

Ella jerked up, feeling her hair tumble further down her back. The trees were like giant buildings surrounding her. Those unusual blue birds hovered between the branches, singing to her in bursts.

She ran after Lore, careful where she was putting her feet.

'What do you mean, although?'

Lore didn't stop. 'There's a gap in your father's memories, which is troubling him. It's almost as if something was taken from his mind.' She glanced at Ella as they strode through the trees. 'Do you know anything about that?'

Ella coughed and scratched at her throat. 'No.'

'Ah, well, a loss is a terrible thing. As you're about to see.'

Ella wondered what Lore was on about until she saw what was in front of them: dozens of dolls hanging from the branches.

'What is this?'

Lore moved to the closest tree, running her fingers over the woollen doll of a young girl.

'This is the Forest of Remembrance for all the children taken by the Kraken.'

They continued and Ella twisted her head to count the dolls, stopping when she reached fifty.

Would I kill the creature to prevent more of this?

By the time she got to the end, she knew what her answer would be.

23 HYMN FROM A VILLAGE

Ella still saw the dolls hanging from the trees as she stepped out of the forest and into the Lorelei village.

'This is where my ancestors settled thousands of years ago.' Lore looked at her. 'And this will be the graveyard of us all unless you can kill the Kraken.'

They stood on a hill overlooking the village, where Ella saw dozens of wooden dwellings on either side of a wide path that cut right through the centre. People moved around at a casual pace as smoke filled the air. About a mile beyond it was the blue of the sea reaching up to the marshmallow clouds filling the sky.

Lore was about to step down the hill when Ella grabbed her arm.

'What was that purple smoke in my world? And where did those creatures come from?'

She let go of her when Lore's tattoos wriggled against her fingers.

'I am the strongest mage of my people. Therefore, conjuring spells of possession are easy for me.'

'You didn't hurt my father when you possessed him?'

'No, child. Come now, there's lots to do in the village before the Kraken returns.'

Lore set off and Ella strode by her side. The land rolled out in front of them like a great green carpet. They walked along a path as Ella placed the gun on her shoulder as if she was some mercenary she'd seen in a TV show where a gunslinger was hired to save poor villagers from a terrible monster.

But what if I'm the monster since my actions led to what has happened to these people?

She tried to push that thought from her head, but it wouldn't go away, oozing at the forefront of her brain as Lore took her into the village. Many villagers were outside, but she didn't see any children, only men and women who had similar tattoos to Lore covering their arms and legs. A few had tattooed faces, and when the illustrations moved, Ella would have sworn the images all stared at her.

The tattoos were mainly of mythological animals, dragons, and sea creatures, but some were of the moon and stars.

But dragons and sea creatures are real, not myths.

The sun painted a yellow sheen across the people as they stopped what they were doing and looked at them. Shadows reached out from the forest behind them and rested over Ella as she entered the village.

A tall grey-haired man carrying a staff approached.

'Welcome home, Lore.' He scrutinised Ella. 'Is this the warrior you promised us?' He gazed at Ella as if she was an ant.

Lore placed her hand on his shoulder. 'Don't worry, Quinn. The girl is tougher than she looks.' She let go of him. 'Have there been more attacks since I left?'

Quinn shook his head. 'Thankfully, no. There's been no sighting of the beast for two days.'

A girl with sparkling blue eyes stood next to Quinn. Ella guessed she was about the same age as her.

'Perhaps the Kraken has left for another land.'

Lore smiled at her. 'Let's hope so, Beatrix. Is Ella's room ready for her?'

Beatrix glanced at Ella. 'It is. Everything you asked for is there.'

'Good, good,' Lore said. 'I'll take her there while you prepare some food. I haven't eaten in an age.'

Beatrix and Quinn turned and headed into the village. The rest of the villagers gathered around them and Ella heard many of them mentioning her name.

She grabbed Lore's arm, ignoring the moving tattoos this time.

'You said you came to Earth to punish me, but that's not true, is it?'

Lore didn't try to escape from her grasp. 'I needed you and I wanted to punish you.'

'I'm a thirteen-year-old girl. What makes you think I can defeat this Kraken?'

'You defeated Pandora the Goddess and left her stranded at the end of the multiverse. The legend of Ella Finn flows through every realm. You are the only one who can kill the Kraken. And you owe us for the damage your actions have caused here.' Lore smiled at her. 'And you'll be fourteen soon.'

Ella took a deep breath. 'Okay, maybe I do have to answer for the consequences of what I've done, but I'm not as strong now as when I defeated Pandora.' She held the gun up. 'All I have is this weapon, and there's no guarantee it'll work here.'

Lore pulled away from her and Ella saw the tattoos on her arm shrink into her skin.

'What do you mean, you're not as strong now?'

'I used Pandora's Light against her, but it's all gone.'

Lore narrowed her eyes. 'You're powerless?'

Ella rubbed one finger over the gun. 'I'm sorry.'

Lore scowled at her as Ella watched all of her tattoos rise from her arms as if they were about to shoot off into the sky. Instead, they hovered in the air, connected to Lore by strands of skin pulling from her body. Ella grimaced at how painful it looked, wondering if the Elemental was going to attack her.

But she didn't.

Instead, she came up with an alternative plan.

'I and some others will give you our Light. You can use that.'

Ella nodded. 'Okay, maybe, but I don't know if that will be enough. Pandora's Light was special because she's the Goddess. I'm not sure if the combined Light of all of your people could replicate that.'

She recognised that to be true, but it wasn't the main motivation for trying to dissuade Lore.

Using Elemental Light is too addictive. I knew it when I took Pandora's from her, and I felt it again when I grabbed that little bit from my cousin near the viaduct.

This was the reason she hadn't used the Book of All Life since returning from the multiverse.

I don't want to turn into an addict.

But what if it's the only way to save Lore and her people from the Kraken?

That thought filled her head as a loud noise burst ahead of them.

She looked towards the sea, astonished to see a great wave rising into the sky.

Lore's face turned dark. 'We're out of time. The beast is coming.'

Ella gripped the gun. 'Then let's meet it.'

She sprinted down the path and through the village, watching as people scattered around her and fled into their houses.

Those bits of wood won't save them. So it's up to me.

Lore ran next to her. 'Do you have a plan?'

As she went, Ella noticed the tattoos swirling into incomprehensible shapes on Lore's body.

'No.'

'Shall I give you my Light?'

She didn't hesitate with her reply. 'No. I'll use this gun to stop the Kraken attacking your community.'

And what if that doesn't work?

They were halfway through the village when they stopped. Ella's feet skidded through the rubble on the path. She looked up to see the water coming towards them like a tsunami.

Maybe it's just a freak tidal wave and the Kraken isn't there.

Then she saw the massive dark shape inside the middle of it.

Lore pulled Ella away as the water split apart and the shadow took on a solid form. The Kraken dropped to the ground as the wave it had ridden washed through the village.

Cold water ran over Ella's shoes and seeped into her feet. The damp bit at her ankles and toes as Lore dragged her into the side of a wooden house.

'Fire your gun now while the beast is getting its bearings.'

Ella stared at the Kraken. Much larger than Lore had

described it before, it was humanoid and covered in grey scales that couldn't hide the huge muscles in its arms and legs. The face was part human, part lion, with a great mane sprouting from its head and reaching down to its massive shoulders. It didn't look at them as it stood from a crouching position and arched its back. Ella guessed it to be maybe three times her size, perhaps fifteen or sixteen feet tall.

Lore whispered to her. 'It's grown since I was here last. Shoot it now while you have the chance.'

Ella raised the gun and put her hand on the trigger.

How do I know what I've been told is true? The Kraken might be an innocent creature and Lore has been lying to me all this time.

But she'd seen those dolls hanging from the trees in the forest, mementoes of children the beast had killed.

If that was the truth.

Seawater squished between her toes as the Kraken turned to them. First, it pushed out its chest, and then eight long, snaking tentacles unfurled from its back. It opened its enormous mouth and Ella smelt death on its breath. Blood dripped from its two great fangs, and she tried not to think of what it had just eaten.

It stared at them through burning red eyes.

And Ella moved towards it. 'What do you want in this village?'

The Kraken blinked and Ella saw tiny fish nibbling at its flesh above the eyes.

Its laughter was like a lion's roar, and water fell from its mouth and bounced over Ella's legs.

'I am the God of this world and I don't answer to children.'

Ella raised the gun so the beast could see what it was.

'And yet you just did.'

The tentacles lifted above the Kraken's head and moved towards her, all slimy and wet.

'I'll eat you first, child, even though there's no meat on you.'

Ella kept looking at the tentacles as they slithered in the air.

Then she took a deep breath and fired the gun.

A laser beam shot out of the weapon, cutting a tentacle in half as the recoil thrust Ella into the building behind her. Her spine cracked against the wood as the Kraken screamed and the smell of burning flesh filled the air.

She had no time to think about the pain shooting through her as another tentacle came for her head. Ella saw the pulsating suckers on the end of it as she rolled to the side. Then she jumped up, ready to fire again, but stopping when she realised Lore had pulled the tentacle to the ground and was slashing at it with a dagger.

'Kill it now, Ella,' Lore shouted as green blood covered her face.

Ella pointed the weapon at the Kraken, but it was too late. A tentacle swept towards her and knocked the gun from her hand. Then another swung round and grabbed her around the waist. The creature lifted her from the ground and pulled Ella to its face.

'I underestimated you, child.' Ella was inches from its head, struggling in its grasp as she watched the green veins shimmering across its skin. 'You're not of this world, are you?' A huge smell of rotten flesh descended on Ella. 'Where are you from?'

Ella saw the gun lying a dozen feet below her and wondered how she could get to it.

'If I tell you, will you let me go?'

The Kraken pushed its face into hers. 'Are they all like you where you come from?'

Ella grimaced at its breath. 'No. I'm the biggest and strongest, the champion of my world.'

All the scales on the Kraken's chest vibrated as it blew out a huge laugh.

'Are there oceans on your world, girl?'

She wriggled in its grasp, but couldn't escape.

'Over seventy per cent of the planet is water.'

The Kraken increased its hold on her. 'How did you get to this world?'

Ella struggled to breathe as she spoke. 'There's a portal near here. I can take you there.'

The beast roared again.

Then it dropped her to the ground.

She hit the earth with a thud, and a stab of electricity shot through her back. Ella bit into her lip, looking around to see the gun a few feet from her. She crawled forward and reached for it.

A great tentacle swooped down and grabbed the weapon. Then the Kraken tossed it into the air. Ella stared at it before it disappeared from view.

Lore came to help her up, with blood dripping from her face as she spoke.

'You're taking the Kraken to your world?'

Ella grimaced at the pain seeping into her bones.

'It's the only way to save your home, Lore.'

'What about yours, Ella Finn?'

Before she could reply, the beast swept her up in a tentacle again.

'Take me to this portal, or I'll devour every living thing in this village.'

So she did.

Because of its great height, the Kraken could crawl through the portal back to Earth. It held Ella in its tentacles as it landed inside the top floor of the Beacon.

It gripped on to her as it scanned its new surroundings.

'You betrayed your home world, child.' It threw her to the side and she bounced across her father's desk, knocking aside the photos of Ella and her family.

The kaleidoscopic light effect of travelling through the portal made her head ache more than landing on the furniture. She rubbed at her eyes as she picked herself up.

'What will you do now?'

The Kraken's tentacles slithered over Ella's skin as it grinned at her.

'I'm going to enjoy myself exploring your world, child. And I'll tell your people what a poor champion you are.' It glanced at the portal shimmering in the wall. 'And when I get bored, I'll return to that other place to start all over again.'

Ella controlled her breathing as the beast strode towards the door, pushing its massive frame against the wood and shattering it. The roar of its laughter beat against her eardrums as she heard it moving down the stairs.

Then she started counting inside her head, waiting for what she knew was coming.

I hope it's coming.

Then it did.

After five seconds. The sound of gunfire. Lots of it.

Ella put her hands over her ears to drown out the noise. And so she couldn't hear the screams of the Kraken.

She didn't know how long she stood like that until she heard someone calling her name.

'It's okay, Ella, you can come down now.'

She stepped over the papers on the floor and through the broken door. She made her way down the stairs, avoiding the green blood on the steps and scrunching up her nose from the smell of death.

She stopped at the bottom where soldiers were covering the Kraken's body with a large plastic sheet.

'Is it dead?' she said to Veronica Venus.

Venus nodded. 'We had no choice. You realise that, right?'

Ella rubbed at the bruise growing on her hip. 'I do.'

She watched them drag the Kraken outside, seeing two of its tentacles sticking out of the tarp and moving over the floor.

'It's a shame about the gun.' Venus said.

'It's a good job you told me there was an open communication device inside of it.'

Veronica Venus smiled at her. 'And it transmitted a live video feed. So we saw and heard everything that happened to you in that other realm.'

'I'm glad you had enough time to get ready, especially with the time difference between there and here.'

'Time difference?' Venus said.

Ella leant against the wall to ease the ache in her legs.

'Half an hour over there is four hours here.' It felt as if the bruise on her hip was spreading across all of her body. 'How long was I gone?'

'Just under eight hours. It was plenty of time to get everything ready for your return.'

'And what if I hadn't come back?'

Veronica Venus moved towards her and took Ella's arm.

'Then I'd have come looking for you. And I would have brought an army with me.' She smiled at her. 'I wouldn't abandon you, Ella.'

Maybe I can work with the Institute after all.

And I can trust Veronica Venus.

Trust her enough to tell her about the Book of All Life.

She let Venus help her outside. It was early morning, with only the street lights providing illumination in the dark; that and the moonlight bouncing off the sea.

Ella thought about Lore and the people of her village.

Perhaps I've done something good.

Venus was leading her to a car when Ella stopped her.

'You better ring my parents to let them know I'm coming home.' To the side of her, she saw the soldiers lifting the dead Kraken into the back of a large truck. 'I hope you gave them a convincing story about where I've been since yesterday.'

Veronica's smile disappeared, replaced by a gloomy shadow covering her face.

'I'm afraid your father isn't at home, Ella. When that Elemental left him, he never regained consciousness.'

Ella heard the words, but didn't hear them.

What she thought she heard was the Kraken's roar as her world turned dark and she collapsed to the ground.

THANK YOU!

Thank you, dear reader for purchasing this book.

If you enjoyed reading about Ella Finn her journey continues in these books:

Ella and the Elementals
Ella and the Multiverse
Ella and the Monsters
Ella and the Dreamers

Many thanks to my wonderful wife for all her support and patience.

Ella and the Monsters edited by Alison Jack.

Extra special thanks to Karina Gallagher for being a dedicated reader of my work.

Cover design by James, GoOnWrite.com

ABOUT THE AUTHOR

Andrew French lives amongst faded seaside glamour on the North East coast of England. He likes gin and cats but not together, new music and old movies, curry and ice cream. Slow bike rides and long walks to the pub are his usual exercise, as well as flicking through the pages of good books and the memoirs of bad people.

Find out more at www.andrewsfrench.com

Facebook:

https://www.facebook.com/A-S-French-Author-150145625006018

Twitter:

www.twitter.com/andrewfrench100

Instagram:

www.instagram.com/andrewfrench100

And replies to all his email at mail@andrewsfrench.com

If you have the time, please leave a review at Amazon or Goodreads

Thank you!